ABSC   ·ION

ADAM CROFT
STEVEN MOORE

Cover photographs © Shutterstock
Designed by Books Covered

PROLOGUE

He descended the steps into Cannon Street tube station, already feeling a world away from his roots. The suited and booted commuters jostled past him as he followed them down towards the westbound platform.

In just a few minutes' time he'd be even further into the beating heart of London, ready to head up the Charing Cross Road and lose himself in the swarming throng as the rucksack he now carried on his back continued on alone along the District Line. He estimated he probably wouldn't even have exited Embankment station by the time the bomb had ripped apart the tube carriage as it rolled into the human chaos of Westminster station.

He wondered how many of the suits would end up in the same carriage as him, how many would still be on the train as it reached Westminster. It would inevitably be a lot, every one of them oblivious to the imminent carnage.

The plan was tight, but controllable. He'd gone through it a thousand times in his head. He'd get on a busy carriage and stand in the gangway, the innocuous rucksack stowed at his feet.

A couple of stops down the line, once the train had left Temple station, he'd bend down and clip the bag shut, as if he'd only just noticed it was undone. At the next stop, Embankment, he'd wait until just before the doors closed before suddenly remembering it was his stop and jumping off the train.

Clipping the bag shut would start the timer, which would reach zero just as the train arrived at Westminster — the heart of government. It was symbolic. Almost poetic. It was a moment that would change history, and for his part in it he would be paid handsomely. What did a few lost suits matter? The city was crawling with them anyway, like rodents. Skimming a few off the top wouldn't hurt.

The District Line train followed the rush of warm air onto the platform and squealed to a halt, hordes of commuters crowding around the doors as they tried to force themselves into the carriage against the effervescent surge of those trying to exit.

He had full control, and knew he could get on any train he wanted, but he wanted to stick to the plan. He saw a space open up and went for it, elbowing his way past a middle-aged woman clutching a Waitrose bag. The look she gave him was pure filth, but he didn't care. She should be thankful she didn't get on the train. Besides which, her view of Muslims would be vindicated, proven and significantly worsened within the next hour.

He tried not to look at any of his fellow passengers as the train departed the station and hurtled down the tracks towards Mansion House. Some of the suits would get off there, ready to start work at any one of a number of investment management companies that lined Queen Victoria Street and the surrounding area. There'd be just as many people getting on, heading further into the centre of London, and a busy train would be good for him. It would reduce the chances of anyone noticing the abandoned rucksack. And, in any case, there would be nothing they could do about it. The doors would be shut, the train would be on its way to Westminster, and the carriage would be blown to pieces before they knew what was happening.

He wiped his brow with the back of his hand. The atmosphere was stifling. The heat of the day didn't help, and he fought to control his nerves. Everything had been planned, everything was under control, yet he still couldn't shake the thought of the rucksack full of explosives currently nestled between his feet.

As expected, a flood of suits got off the train at Mansion House, only to be replaced by more suited clones. He closed his eyes and counted his breaths to ten, before repeating the exercise over and over again.

Time seemed to take an age to pass, but as the train rolled into Temple station, he shuffled slightly to the side in order to give himself room to bend down and clip the rucksack shut. As the last passengers got on and the door closed with a whoosh, he swallowed hard. He took his opportunity — the jolt of the accelerating train — to look down at the rucksack, before bending over and, with a deep breath, securing the clip.

That was it. There was no going back now. In four minutes, the rucksack would no longer exist. Neither would most of the people on the carriage, obliviously reading their newspapers or listening to music as the fireball tore through them.

He looked at his watch. Almost a minute had passed. Within seconds they'd be at Embankment and he'd make a rush for the exit. Then there'd be just two minutes to go.

His heart lurched as he felt the train slow down, much earlier than he'd expected.

They were still in a tunnel.

No. No, no no. This wasn't happening. It couldn't stop now. Not here. He had to get off. He wasn't meant to be on the train when the timer hit zero. That wasn't part of the plan.

He looked around him for a way out. Would the doors open in a tunnel? In any case, how would he get far enough away from the train to avoid being killed by the blast?

He squeezed his eyes shut and prayed to Allah for the train to move. After what seemed like an age, but according to his watch was barely ten seconds, he felt the train start to move again.

They were moments away from Embankment, and he needed to get off the train fast.

It began to slow as he saw the white tiles flashing past the windows. He desperately wanted to stand by the doors and dart straight out when they opened, but he knew he had to stay on the spot until that moment. He couldn't risk giving some do-gooder the opportunity to let him know he'd left his rucksack behind.

As the train jolted to a halt, there followed a brief pause before the doors opened with a whoosh. He counted to five, then pushed his way through the crowd of commuters and up towards the escalators.

1

An audible buzz permeated the office. Most staff and supervisors seemed agitated, some from excitement, others due to nerves and stress. They all knew there was an important visitor touring their section of the Home Office that morning, and it added a little spark to an otherwise dreary late spring day in London.

Sam Barker sat behind his desk, sipping his coffee and appraising the mood of his colleagues. It was always interesting to see people's reactions whenever a high-profile politician visited the office. Granted, usually it was the current Home Secretary or occasionally even the Prime Minister, but today's visitor was Michael Sullivan, leader of Her Majesty's official opposition, who was widely expected to become the next Prime Minister following the imminent general election.

Following the introduction of the Fixed Term Parliaments Act in 2010, the next election was due in around two months, and there didn't seem to be any sign of Sullivan's support waning. If anything, his predicted share of the vote was growing by the day.

Sullivan had picked his ailing party off the floor after being almost wiped out in a general election landslide a few years earlier. The political landscape had shifted hugely, and Sullivan had built support not by the traditional method of appealing to the political centre ground, but by harnessing the media's stoking of societal tensions and building a populist, nationalist movement which appealed to many Britons' desire for a certain kind of stability and return to traditional values.

Sam wasn't keen on outside visitors himself. He much preferred to be able to stick to his usual daily routine, without worrying about any interference from outside or having to deal with the unexpected. He hoped Sullivan wouldn't want to speak to him. Although he certainly had nothing against the man — far from it — he really wasn't keen on having to speak to strangers, and he felt that more than ever as the cuticle on his right thumb started to bleed where he'd torn away the skin with his teeth.

When it came to Sullivan himself, Sam admired the man's desire to keep Britain safe and had noticed he was often the first politician to denounce atrocities in the media — often before the Prime Minister himself. Whatever anyone said about his politics, Sullivan was clearly a leader, and that was something Sam believed Britain needed.

Eleven o'clock came around and, as expected, Michael Sullivan entered the office, escorted by Sam's boss, Frank Anderson. Sam and Frank weren't exactly close colleagues — not that Sam ever really got close to anyone. Frank knew Sam was a valuable member of the team, however, and let him get on with things, much to Sam's pleasure. Sam only wished that was how Frank treated all his colleagues.

Frank was a tall, puffy man in his early fifties, fortunate still to have a head full of dirty-blonde hair, less fortunate that he had not one clue how to style it. If Sam didn't know better, and Boris Johnson wasn't so stumpy, they might have been brothers.

But Sam knew that — other than his less-than-discreet but futile attempts at flirting with every female in the office — Frank was good at his job, and was a fair and well-respected boss. But that didn't mean Sam had to like him.

As Frank and Michael Sullivan approached Sam's area of the office, they stopped to chat with Lucy Jones, one of only a few people Sam considered a friend — not only in the office but beyond the confines of work, too.

Lucy was pretty, and her bubbly nature endeared her to everyone she met. She wasn't immune to a little flirting herself, and Sam watched on as she caught Sullivan's full attention. They were out of Sam's range and he couldn't hear what was said, but Sullivan and Frank Anderson left Lucy to her work after a minute of chatting.

The very nature of Sam's work as a civil servant meant he was — and had to be — completely impartial. His job was to do the bidding of the government of the day, whoever happened to be leading it. But, naturally, everyone had their own political opinions and leanings.

Sam had always considered himself to be patriotic, and sometimes wondered what had happened to traditional British values. Although he didn't support any party in particular, he could see how Sullivan managed to cultivate his widespread appeal and understood the demographic which appeared to be most likely to vote for him.

Sullivan and Frank edged nearer Sam's desk and Frank introduced him.

'This is Sam Barker, one of our cyber security team,' Frank

said. 'It's a wide-ranging remit, and one which is constantly changing with the political landscape, but he's one of our best, without a doubt.'

Sullivan nodded and smiled at Sam. 'Nice to meet you, Simon. Good work.'

And with that, Sullivan had moved further down the office, where he was already engaging in lengthy conversation with one of Sam's young female colleagues.

Sam glanced up and saw Lucy looking at him. She pursed her lips, which Sam translated as a look of sympathy. Sam breathed deeply and turned towards his computer screen as Lucy walked over.

'What was that all about?' Lucy whispered, stating the obvious and adding a knowing wink.

Sam couldn't help but smile. 'No idea. People get names wrong all the time. It's fine. He's a busy guy.'

Lucy and Sam had got on well since she'd first started in the office a year or two ago. Other than Sam's girlfriend, Dee, who worked as an HR manager, Lucy was the only other staff member Sam trusted enough to have a laugh with. If it wasn't for Dee, Sam wondered if there might have been something between him and Lucy. As it was, the three of them were good friends, and Sam knew the girls would have a laugh at Sam's expense in the pub after work tonight.

Sullivan eventually left the office at midday. Sam knew why he'd come. As leader of the opposition, and if — as expected — his party was to win the upcoming general election, Sullivan would become Prime Minister and effective head of all government departments. He was there purely to try and win the hearts and minds of what he considered his future employees. And, for the most part, he seemed to be succeeding.

Later that day, Sam was starting to wrap up for the week. He'd closed down all his open files and browser tabs on his computer and tidied up his desk. He'd taken his coffee cup and plate through to the office's small kitchenette and washed them ready for Monday morning.

Sam needed to have things things neat and organised. He was the same at home. If things were untidy, Sam couldn't focus. *Tidy house, tidy mind*, his mother had always said. As a result, his modest flat in Waterloo was spotless and impeccably ordered.

It was just another way in which his inherent anxiety manifested itself. If everything was clean, tidy and organised, he felt a little more ready to conquer the world — not that he ever conquered any bits of it other than his short walk to work and the occasional drinks in the pub with one or two chosen work colleagues.

He'd already emailed Lucy and Dee to confirm the location for tonight's drinks, and Sam could almost taste the beer when at five o'clock that Friday afternoon the email alert on his monitor pinged seconds before he would have shut it down. Glancing at the screen, his heart sank when he realised he'd been summoned into an immediate meeting with Frank Anderson.

Wanting to get it over and done with, he walked over towards Frank's office. Taking a deep breath, Sam knocked and entered without waiting. Frank neither spoke nor looked up for long moments and, when he finally did, Sam spotted a smug look on his face.

'Sam. I'll cut to the chase.'

Sam's pulse quickened. There was something in the way Frank was looking at him that set alarm bells ringing.

'We're having to refocus some of our efforts here over the coming weeks and months. There's a bit of a shift of direction happening, and internal security will be leant on much more heavily than usual. As a result we're having to cut annual leave for our most important staff.'

'Cut it?'

'For now. You'll still be able to take it, but at the end of the annual cycle.'

'But there are already things booked. I'm meant to be going to Edinburgh to see my son.'

Frank shuffled awkwardly. 'If there are short breaks already arranged, and if there's evidence that the travel arrangements and accommodation have already been booked and paid for, we can make exceptions. But no future leave will be authorised until further notice.'

Sam's heart sank. He hadn't arranged any travel for Edinburgh yet, so would fall foul of that little loophole. The thought of not being able to see Benji again until further notice was heartbreaking.

He didn't get to see his son anywhere near as often as he would have liked, but it could never have been any other way. He and Benji's mum were not far off his age when they met, and — looking back — there was no way it was ever going to be a long-term relationship. Falling pregnant had been a mistake, but Sam knew instantly that he had to step up and be a father.

The day Leila told him she was pregnant, Sam Barker grew up. He'd never been the most confident child, but he gained a deep and immediate desire to make sure his child had the best possible start in life. When Leila's parents decided they were moving the whole family back to Scotland, Sam was torn apart inside, but ultimately knew not to argue. Instead, he'd spent every waking hour earning a crust and every spare moment travelling back and forth from Edinburgh to visit him.

He and Leila had remained good friends, too. She told him once over a boozy lunch that she'd seen a couple of her friends falling pregnant at a young age and being abandoned by the fathers of their children. Sam, on the other hand, had chosen to do the right thing and Leila respected him for that.

He wondered if perhaps he'd be able to get up there and back within a weekend. The train journey usually took anywhere between four and a half and five hours, so it might be doable for a one-night stay. He'd have to look into it. Anything would be worth it just to spend a few hours with Benji.

Sam could find no words to say to Frank. There had been rumours for weeks that things were going to be changing, not just in his office, but across all Home Office departments. It was usual for incoming governments to want to change things, and Sam and his colleagues were used to the ground shifting beneath them every couple of years when a new Home Secretary decided a 'shake up' was what was needed. But Sullivan wasn't yet the Prime Minister.

It didn't make sense, and Sam wanted answers, but he couldn't find the right questions or pluck up the courage to ask them, and Frank sat back in his chair, his eyes locked on Sam's. Sam's problem was Frank knew he wasn't at all the combative type. Frank considered Sam meek. Quiet. Diligent in his work. Uber-talented, for sure. But he must have known Sam would acquiesce without argument.

'We'll let you all know when things change, Sam.'

Sam returned to his desk, a mix of emotions swelling in his mind. His girlfriend Dee approached, sensing something was up. It was after five, and time to get the hell out of there.

'Tell me about it over a pint?' she asked.

Sam looked up at Dee, but his usual smile wasn't forthcoming.

'Oh dear. What's happened? What did Frank want?'

Sam blinked. 'Let's hit the pub.'

Twenty minutes later, Sam, Dee and Lucy had tucked themselves into a corner booth of the pub. It was low-key, and other than it being just two minutes' walk from his flat, the best thing for Sam was that he'd never seen anyone else from his work there. Regardless, he scanned the room as he sat there, making himself familiar with his surroundings and trying to lower his anxiety, all whilst avoiding potential eye contact with any strangers.

'So you're not going to get to see Benji again any time soon?' Dee asked.

'Doesn't look like it. There's no way he can get down here on his own, not with how busy he is at uni. He's got back-to-back lectures and assignments.'

'They can't just cancel annual leave. That's outrageous.' Lucy was genuinely shocked. She thought she knew everything that went on in their office, but she hadn't seen that one coming. Nor had anyone else.

'That's what I thought, but hey. I'll just have to go up for a few hours on weekends or something.'

Dee wasn't quite as optimistic. 'It's just so unfair. I mean, why you? Why now?'

'Honestly, I don't know. Apparently it's just certain roles.'

'You'd think that might be something I'd have heard about,' Dee said. 'I suppose HR are the last to know.'

'I'll see if I can find anything out,' Lucy replied. 'You know I can bend Frank round my little finger.' It was true. If anyone could extract information from their boss, it was Lucy. 'Another round?' she asked, though as far as rhetorical questions went, that was right up there.

The three of them had gone for drinks after work on a Friday almost every week for the last twelve months, and a tight bond had formed between them. It was one of the ways in which Sam had learned to manage aspects of his anxiety. Although the social aspect was an issue, it was also a routine — and one which he cherished.

Lucy left the booth and headed for the bar, drawing the gaze of more than a few male patrons.

Dee scooted a little closer to Sam. They had been seeing each other for almost three years now. They got on brilliantly, trusted each other implicitly and enjoyed the fact that they were both comfortable about not getting too serious. At least not yet.

For a while, Sam had been considering discussing with Dee about taking things up a level. He didn't want to get engaged or commit to anything just yet, but he enjoyed Dee staying over at his flat and thought it might be a logical next step for her to move in. He hadn't quite found the moment to ask, though. In fact, in recent months Sam felt that — if anything — Dee might even have been drifting a little. She had often seemed distracted and a little bit of the spark had gone from her eyes. Sam had asked her about it a few times.

'Just a little stressed with work, bit more tired than usual, that's all,' she'd answer. 'Don't worry about it.' Sam hadn't been all that convinced, and had found Dee a little bit too dismissive. But he didn't want to push it.

If true, though, it was understandable. Dee's job as Human Resources manager at the Home Office was tough, and though she worked from home a couple of days a week, Sam knew she worked long hours.

'You should stand up to him, you know. Frank,' Dee said. 'You can't keep letting people push you around like this.'

'No-one's pushing me around,' Sam replied, swilling the remainder of his pint around the bottom of the glass. 'It's workable. If things are changing and they need the manpower, that's understandable.'

'It's not right, Sam.'

'It's fine. I don't want to rock the boat.'

Lucy returned with the drinks and squashed back into the booth. 'That Sullivan's a little slimy, isn't he? Couldn't take his eyes off my, uh... you know?'

'He's a politician... they're all like that,' confirmed Dee.

'That's not fair,' said Sam. 'Not all. There's nothing wrong with being friendly.'

Sam would have to concede that he was a little old-school, and his faith in the system of government remained strong, despite growing unease across Britain in recent years. The nation's mistrust in government ratcheted up several notches after the lies told by Tony Blair under his 'New Labour' government, when he led Britain into an illegal war in the Gulf in 2003. The country's trust in their politicians had never really recovered, and successive governments, both Labour and Conservative, had done nothing to appease those doubts — at least not for most people. But Sam remained staunch in his patriotism. He wanted to believe in the system. He needed to. It gave him deep comfort.

'Still,' said Lucy, 'it doesn't hurt to make friends in high places, eh?'

'No, I guess not,' Sam said.

Dee had been quiet most of the evening, and half an hour later she surprised both Sam and Lucy with her decision to leave the pub so early. 'Sorry guys. Just not feeling great.' She looked at Sam. 'Call me tomorrow?'

'Sure thing. You okay? Can I walk you home?'

'I'm good, thanks. Just going to snag a cab and have an early night. Chat tomorrow.'

Sam stood and pecked Dee on the cheek. It was unlike Dee to be so aloof, but he didn't want to push it and shrugged at Lucy as they watched Dee leave the bar.

'She okay, you think?' asked Lucy.

'Not sure, to be honest. She's been under pressure at work lately, but I have to admit she hasn't quite been herself for a while. I'll see her tomorrow, see if I can find out what's up. Anyway, my round?'

Lucy smiled. 'Thought you'd never ask.'

2

TWO WEEKS AGO

'Looking forward to tomorrow?' Jason Collins asked, placing down Sam's pint, having already sunk half of his own. They didn't see each other as much as they used to, but they had remained close and it was always good to catch up.

'I am, thanks. It's been almost two months since I've seen him. Guess I'm a little nervous.'

Sam missed his son dearly and travelled north to visit as often as he could, which unfortunately wasn't often enough. He and Leila had both regretted it when she'd fallen pregnant. They were young and naive, and it was a stupid mistake. But they both soon changed their minds when Benji was born. Leila was a great mother, and despite her and Sam parting soon after — for the best, they both agreed — she'd raised a well-grounded young man.

If he was being honest, Sam missed Leila too. But they had different lives now, and in Leila's case Sam was certain that at least she, if not Benji, was better off without him.

Sam had known Jason since they were children. By chance

they had attended the same university, though had read different subjects. Jason studied political science, while Sam had studied information technology focusing on computer networks, digital forensics and cyber security, resulting in his job at the Home Office.

Neither had played sport in university, though both enjoyed watching the odd game in the pub these days. Today's offering was a friendly match between England and Spain, which was going surprisingly well for the home team, just down the road at Wembley Stadium.

Sam rarely missed an England match on TV, whether rugby, football or cricket, despite the years of disappointments. Back at uni, when Sam had successfully used alcohol as a crutch for his social anxiety, they had enjoyed going to the almost-nightly music gigs on campus, some of the acts well-known bands, others made up of hopeful students. Sam would argue, tongue in cheek, that he was there strictly for the music. Jason, on the other hand, had no shame admitting he was there for the drinking and the girls. He was successful at both endeavours, something Sam had admired with a certain well-hidden jealousy. It was that familiarity of knowing someone from their hometown as they moved away from their parents for the first time that had kept their relationship afloat throughout those early years, and later, when they'd both located back to London.

And in a world that was, it seemed to Sam, reverting to a darker, near-apocalyptic time, where high-level corruption, terrorism and violent events made up the bulk of the daily news, familiarity was something Sam was grateful for.

'Yeah, I won't be out late tonight. Getting the seven-thirty to Edinburgh in the morning.'

'Seven-thirty?' Jason chuckled, well aware England's shoddy public transport system was always ready to let you down. 'Good luck with that leaving on time. Dee going with you?'

'Yep. Making a long weekend of it.'

'Isn't it a little, erm, awkward? I mean, with Dee and Leila?' he asked.

'Not at all. They get on great. In fact, they're in more regular contact than me and Leila. Probably gossiping about how dull I am.'

'You are pretty dull, it has to be said,' Jason said, never shy about dishing out the banter.

'Wow. And they say honesty's always the best policy. Still pushing bits of paper around for a living?'

'Someone's got to do it. Without logistics planners nothing happens, you know.'

'Sounds dull to me,' Sam replied.

'It really isn't,' Jason said, chuckling.

'Well, if it's so important, it must be well paid. Mine's a pint.'

Dee had texted Sam at the last minute to say she wouldn't be able to come to Edinburgh after all. While Sam was disappointed, it meant he'd get to spend time alone with his son, and that was fine with him.

Dee hadn't told Sam exactly why she couldn't come with him, but it was just the latest in a growing list of out-of-character moments that had Sam worried. He knew she was fiercely independent, and he admired that about her. For the first couple of years since they'd met, though, she would never have cancelled so late in the day. It was yet another sign that her mind was elsewhere — and not on him. *Then again, why would it be?* he thought as he boarded the early Virgin train to Edinburgh out of Euston.

Sam had ended up staying in the pub later than planned the previous night. Jason had a way of doing that — something Sam recalled had happened far too often over the years, but which had allowed Sam to temporarily mute his anxieties with alcohol. He rested his throbbing head back against the seat and stared out of the window as the train eased its way out of London on time, picking up pace and soon speeding north.

He realised he must've fallen fast asleep, because before he knew it, Sam opened his eyes to find the train heading over the wide curving bridge that crossed the river at Berwick-upon-Tweed, which meant they were only forty-five minutes from Edinburgh. Benji should be there to meet him at Waverley Station, and Sam sensed that familiar twist of anxiety in his gut. He knew he shouldn't feel nervous, but he couldn't help it. He had split up with Leila when Benji was less than a year old, and though it was an amicable decision to break up, he had always retained a hefty dose of guilt for not being there much during Benji's younger years.

For Benji's part, he coped just fine, and loved the fact his dad lived in London and that he got to visit with his friends sometimes, whenever uni allowed. Nevertheless, Sam's guilt was constant, and was only tempered by the infinite love he felt for his son. As he stepped from the train at Waverley and spotted Benji waiting at the barrier, his heart leapt with pride.

'Hi Dad. You look, uh... hungover?'

Sam grabbed Benji in a tight hug and didn't respond to the friendly jibe. After a few seconds, Benji eased away from him, and Sam realised for the first time that his son was now taller than him.

'What on earth's your mum feeding you? You must be six foot already.'

'Six two, actually. Shorty.'

Sam chuckled. 'Usual?'

'Sounds good.'

Sam and Benji left Waverley Station and rode the escalators up to Princes Street, where they turned right and made a beeline for Benji's favourite lunch spot, Rabbi's Café Bar. After ordering — a chicken sandwich for Sam and a vegan wrap for Benji — they fell into easy conversation.

'Vegan?' Sam loved animals, but he didn't understand how anyone could give up meat.

'Yep. It's good on so many levels, Dad. The barbaric animal farming industry, obviously. But the environment. Global warming. It's all related to people eating meat. People have to know how damaging it is.'

Sam was listening to Benji, but his words paled under the immense pride and love he felt for his son, who was fast-becoming a smart, handsome man of the world — much more of the world, Sam suspected, than he'd ever been.

'Dad? You even listening?'

'Yeah, course I am. You're telling me about meat.'

Benji shook his head. 'Yeah, and how you shouldn't eat it.'

Sam looked at his half-finished sandwich and grinned. 'Sorry. I'll try and eat less. So, how's uni going?'

Benji told his dad about the classes on his environmental science course at the University of Edinburgh. He'd only started in September, but he was clearly revelling in it and Sam could tell his son was inspired to make a difference.

'Hey, so there's a Global Warming Summit taking place here at Edinburgh Castle later this year. Me and some friends from uni are gonna go and protest. Why don't you come up and support us? You might even learn something.' Benji was teasing, but Sam suspected his son genuinely meant it. He'd see if he could make it, but he knew he always had the get-out clause of having to remain politically impartial — not to mention being unable to do anything unless it was a weekend.

Later that day, Benji introduced Sam to his friend, a pretty girl he'd met at uni and who Sam suspected was more than just a friend. Later still, Leila joined them for dinner, and Sam wasn't at all surprised to hear how disappointed she was Dee couldn't make it.

'I'm not sure why she cancelled, to be honest. She's been a little distant lately.'

Leila offered a sympathetic smile. 'Is everything okay with you two? I mean, she's lovely, Sam. Make sure you keep hold of her.'

Sam's eyebrows and shoulders rose in unison, as if to say *It's out of my hands*, but he was glad to know Leila still cared about him and that she wished him well. That meant a lot to Sam, but more importantly it was good for their son.

The rest of the weekend passed in a blur of impassioned environmental-awareness speeches by Benji as they shopped, hiked around the beautiful Arthur's Seat in the east of the city and generally enjoyed some quality father-son time together. And it was with a heavy heart that they parted, but not before lunch on Sunday, when — under duress — Sam ordered his first ever vegan dinner. He was shocked at how good it was, and he boarded the train back to London with a promise to return for the environmental summit in a few months' time.

He only hoped Dee would still be around to join him.

3

ONE WEEK AGO

Sam's heart sank as he double-checked and triple-checked the small fridge in his flat. There was definitely no milk.

He remembered using the last of it yesterday morning, but was certain he'd ordered it on his weekly shop, which had turned up earlier that morning.

He pulled the printed receipt out of the recycling bin and scanned it, looking for a mention of milk. There was nothing. He'd forgotten to order it. And it was a Sunday. The café downstairs would be closed, so he couldn't just pop down and buy a bottle from Emma, the owner.

His heart started to beat faster and more prominently in his chest as he realised he was going to have to go out and get some. There were two things that made Sam particularly anxious: having to go out in public any more than was necessary, and his plans being changed for him.

He'd had it all laid out in his mind. He was going to make himself a cup of tea, sit down in front of the TV, still in his dressing gown, and watch whatever film happened to be on the first movie channel he came across. It didn't sound like much, but that was to be his Sunday morning and he'd decided on it. Now he was going to have to get dressed and go out to get some milk, or he wouldn't be able to have tea or even a bowl of cereal later in the day. To many people it might have sounded like a small inconvenience, but for Sam it was horribly anxiety inducing.

He closed his eyes and swallowed, trying to calm his nerves. *It's only a pint of milk,* he told himself. *The shop is right round the corner. You know every step of the way.* He knew, logically speaking, it was ridiculous. He didn't need anyone to tell him that. But that still didn't change the way he thought and felt, nor did it help him in any way. His anxiety was an automatic reaction to certain situations, and it was as much a part of him as his hair or his right ankle.

He went into his bedroom and slipped on a short-sleeved shirt and some trousers, before putting on his socks and shoes and heading for his front door. He took a deep breath, unlocked the latch and stepped out onto the landing, closing the door behind him.

His walk to the Tesco Express on Baylis Road would take him two, maybe three minutes. He hoped the fresh air would help the rising panic, but he couldn't bank on it. His stress levels had been higher than usual recently, and that tended to result in his anxiety coming on faster and heavier than it otherwise might.

Before long he reached the shop, walking inside and making his way straight over to the milk section. He picked up four pints of full-fat — more than he would need, but it would ensure he didn't need to do this again — and turned to head towards the checkouts. As he did, a voice called out to him.

'Sam!'

He vaguely recognised it, but couldn't place it. It was friendly, familiar, but he still wanted to get the hell out of here and back into his flat.

'Sam, how's it going?' the voice said, closer now. He looked up to see Yasmin, the wife of Malik, who worked in the café below his flat.

'Hi. Sorry, in a world of my own,' Sam replied, smiling, not being entirely untruthful.

'Don't worry, I've been the same recently. But seeing as I've bumped into you, I should probably tell you. I'm pregnant,' she beamed. 'We're expecting a baby.'

Sam was pulled from his reverie, a genuine smile spreading across his face. 'Wow. That's fantastic news. Congratulations. You must be over the moon.'

'We are,' Yasmin said, a warm glow in her eyes. 'We're going to tell all our friends and family later today, actually. We had the twelve-week scan yesterday.'

'That's amazing,' Sam said. As far as he was concerned, it couldn't have happened to a nicer couple. 'That must put the due date somewhere around Christmas, right?'

'Yep, a couple of weeks before. Going to be an expensive time of year from now on!'

'Definitely. Although I guess it gets all the present-buying out of the way in one go,' Sam said, now having run to the limits of his small-talk capabilities.

Yasmin grinned again, then threw her arms around Sam, who stood awkwardly, unsure what to do.

'Sorry,' she said, finally letting go of him. 'Truth be told, you're the first person to find out. Don't tell anyone that, obviously. But I had to tell you, especially seeing as you were right here.'

'No, of course,' Sam replied. 'I won't tell a soul. Your families will be made up, I'm sure.'

'Mum especially,' Yasmin said. 'She's been asking us for ages when we were planning to start a family. I can't wait to see the look on her face.'

4

TODAY

Sam locked the door of his modest flat and descended the narrow creaking staircase to the street below, easing past the racing bike stored at the bottom of the stairs.

'Bollocks!' he muttered, as the bike fell away from the wall and almost tripped him up. He paused, sucking in a deep breath and exhaling slowly through his nostrils, trying not to get annoyed. The battle with the bicycle was daily, and served as a constant reminder to Sam that he couldn't afford to move anywhere better than his rented one-bedroom flat above the Travelling Through bookshop café in Waterloo. The bike wasn't even his. It was Emma's, the owner of the business. Emma was also his landlady, and part of his rental agreement was that she could store her bike in his hallway whenever she was working in the shop. He hadn't realised just how much it would annoy him, and even after years of living there Sam still wasn't used to it.

Nevertheless, if that was the most annoying part of his day, Sam knew his life was okay. Ordinary, for sure, but it could be a lot worse. The fact he couldn't take his annual leave whenever he wanted gnawed at him a little, but he tried to stay positive about that and remain focused on his job, despite his boss.

With thoughts of his visit to see Benji fresh in his mind, he stepped out into a sunny Lower Marsh Road. He hadn't eaten yet, nor drunk any coffee, and he turned directly into Emma's café, hoping she was tucked away in her office. He had neither the time nor the desire to listen to her rambling on about everything and nothing this morning, and it was usually both.

'Morning, buddy.' It was Malik, one of the members of staff at Travelling Through.

'Hello mate,' said a relieved Sam. 'You okay?'

'Can't complain, thanks. Usual?' Malik asked, though it was a rhetorical question. Sam smiled.

'How'd you know?' He'd been ordering his customary cappuccino and cinnamon-topped Danish pastry from Malik almost every work day for the last six months, ever since Malik had first started at the café.

'How's Yasmin?' Sam asked.

'Oh, you know. Pretty good, ta. Busy working a lot of overtime these days, what with the baby coming around Christmas. In fact she's just left here, probably five minutes ahead of you. She's heading over to Ealing to see her mum.'

Sam smiled. 'Her mum must be over the moon with it all.'

Malik beamed. 'Yeah, she is. She's practically counting down the hours, never mind the weeks. Here's your breakfast, mate. Have a good day.'

'Thanks, you too. Give my regards to Yasmin.'

'Will do. And Sam?'

Sam turned back to his friend. 'What's up?'

'Take care, man,' Malik said, adding a friendly wink.

Sam grinned and headed off to work, opting to take the

slightly longer route to the Home Office by crossing Westminster Bridge. He almost always chose this route, especially when the weather was good. He felt an immense sense of innate pride every time he crossed the bridge and saw the Houses of Parliament, Big Ben and Westminster Cathedral that dominated the iconic London skyline. To Sam, there simply was no better city in the world on a sunny day.

Despite the prospect of yet another routine shift stuck behind his desk, he strode west with purpose, negotiating the daily throngs. It was a chaotic mix of commuters and eager tourists, most of whom were focused on their mobile phones and ignoring the majestic, shimmering curves of the Thames as it snaked below them from its source two-hundred miles west. Sam had never understood that modern phenomenon, where tourists spent thousands of pounds travelling to a place but were more preoccupied with posing for selfies than admiring what the destination was famous for. *Maybe I'm just getting old*, he thought, and smiled.

Sam reached the end of Westminster Bridge and angled west towards the Home Office building, then stopped short. *Bollocks*, he thought for the second time already that morning. Sam suddenly remembered it was Lucy's birthday, and he'd forgotten to buy her anything. Lucy was one of the few people in Sam's office, other than those that relied on him on an almost-hourly basis, who even registered his existence. If he didn't show up at work today clutching a present, she'd never let him hear the end of it.

On a whim, Sam hustled across Great George Street on the corner of Parliament Square, and ducked down the steps into Westminster Underground station. He knew there was a florist on the lower concourse. Thinking back, he thought he might have bought Lucy flowers last year, but he didn't have time for anything better right now, and silently cursed his memory. Dodging left and right against the irresistible flow of the exiting crowds, trying to remain calm, he found his way to the florist, where a huge man greeted him with a broad Jamaican accent and an even broader, knowing grin.

'Morning! You forget something?' he asked, noticing how hard Sam had worked to get to his stall.

'Something like that,' Sam said, breathing hard now, concerned he'd be late for work, something he'd never been in all his time in the civil service. 'I'll take those, please,' he said, pointing to a colourful bunch of flowers he couldn't possibly name. 'How much?'

'Fifteen quid, buddy. Hope she's worth it.'

Sam nodded and thanked the man as he handed him the flowers. Fifteen quid was definitely worth it to preserve the peace. Sam turned and swallowed hard as he tried to force back his panic and head for the exits.

5

Sam had been on the London Underground before, but he was far from keen on it and tried to avoid it whenever possible. It was busy, often overcrowded and he felt a deep sense of claustrophobia every time he had to descend those steps.

He knew it would be easier if he stayed calm, but it wasn't always that easy. Sam felt uneasy at the rumbling of the concrete floors, thanks to the hundreds of thousands of footsteps pounding through the tunnels between the various platforms, as well as the roar of the train carriages vibrating far below in that vast underground world.

Occasionally, when he felt his anxiety starting to get out of control, he'd force himself to get the tube to work — or to wherever he needed to go — just to keep everything at bay and to show himself he was capable of doing it. It was one way of stopping his anxiety from taking over completely, which could be devastating.

He didn't want to be here today, but this was the only place he knew he could get a bunch of flowers quickly and relatively cheaply. Besides which, he didn't have to actually get on a train

— the stall was on the concourse, which meant he could now get back up above ground and onto his usual route to work in no time at all. Not far now, then he'd be back out on the street again.

Sam's stride shortened just then, his eyes suddenly widening as he slowed down amid the throng. Then they narrowed in concentration as he came to a standstill. Something felt different. A variant on the usual deep throb and rumble of the concourse. Intangible, but present.

He felt it all before he heard it. The vibrations beneath his feet. The shaking of the concourse walls. The collective tensing of muscles all around him, herding together, as if everyone knew what it was but were momentarily frozen, unable to move or think or breathe.

Then came that screeching, whooshing noise that morphed into a percussive, slowly-building roar which lasted just a few seconds, only to be replaced by a deafening, frightening boom that was all encompassing, a sound so incredibly loud it swallowed Sam whole, as if forever.

Darkness. Total darkness. An earthly blackhole. Oppressive weight on him, crushing his body, squeezing the air from his lungs. Wringing him out.

And then the silence. The vacuum of noise was strange, unnatural. After the unbelievable sound just moments ago, it was surreal.

All Sam could hear at first was nothing. Then his own ragged breaths, wheezy from inhaling dry, clogging dust. Slowly the silence faded. Snippets of sound. Noises. They grew louder, closer. The grinding of concrete against concrete, the twisting of steel. He smelled sulphur, as if in the aftermath of nearby fireworks, and the distinctive metallic smell of sparklers or welding. Singed clothes and hair. Burned skin.

And the unmistakable sound of human suffering.

Agonised groans of pain. Cries of disbelief. Anguish. Horror. Shock.

Lying still, Sam took a mental inventory of his injuries. Nothing. Nothing hurt. Not too much, anyway. He tried shifting his weight off his right side, then grimaced in agony, clenching his teeth hard together, instantly nauseous. He knew then he'd broken ribs, or at least fractured a couple. It wasn't lethal, but it really fucking hurt. He eased cautiously onto his back, each stilted breath agony, and tried to free his arms. After he'd managed that, he reached out into the darkness, assessing his predicament. Slivers of light penetrated the rubble, and he pushed against something with his palms, forcing it up and away. He was afraid bigger, deadlier chunks of masonry or concrete might fall, but nothing did. Light spilled into the opening and he saw blood, unsure if it was his. He didn't think it was. A fit of coughing erupted from his throat, dust and saliva mixing and dribbling down his chin.

He sat up, squinting against the light. With horror, Sam realised he wasn't on the lower concourse now. Well, technically he was, but the lower concourse had moved. Instead of the Jamaican florist, he saw what looked like tracks. The ground had literally opened up below him and the many hundreds of commuters, and deposited them in a massive, mangled and crumpled heap on the platform below. He glanced around in disbelief. Then he saw it. What was once the crowded carriage of a London Underground train was now a destroyed, warped and flaming tomb to dozens and dozens of slain victims. Innocent, unsuspecting victims.

Sam now registered fully for the first time what had happened. An explosion. A bombing on the Underground. Westminster, one of London's busiest tube stations. At rush hour. 'Fuck,' he muttered, noticing in the shafts of light flecks of blood expelled with his breath. 'Fucking hell.'

Sam scrambled to his feet and saw other figures around him, silhouettes on the dimly lit platform. Some standing, others crouched. More on the ground, some moving. Still more weren't moving.

Dead.

Sam was now in tremendous pain, but he could still move, and he set about looking for survivors. There remained enough residual light to see, and he clambered out of his near-tomb and began looking. Others helped too, and within minutes the emergency services were on the scene, leading the search and rescue effort. For an hour Sam cautiously combed the rubble, ultimately assisting in escorting more than a dozen injured people onto the tracks and away from the burning carriage. Fire officers now had the blaze under control, but Sam hoped whoever had done this was on that carriage. He hoped they were dead.

'Sam?'

Sam froze. Had he heard that correctly? Had someone called his name?

'Sam. S-Sam, can you... help —'

He heard it clearly then, but didn't recognise the scratchy female voice. 'Where are you?' he called. 'I can't see you.'

'H-here.'

Sam clambered over piles of rubble towards the voice, then paused to listen.

'Help.'

The plea was little more than a croak, and Sam knew

whoever had said it was in a world of pain. There! He spotted a hand resting against concrete. Brown skin. Asian, probably, and a knot tightened in his gut. Malik's words flitted through his mind.

She's just left here. Probably five minutes ahead of you.

No. It was an irrational thought. Thousands of brown-skinned women were using the Underground that morning. But...

'I'm here,' he said. 'I'm going to help.' Sam eased onto the concrete next to the hand and assessed the situation. The woman was trapped, that was obvious, but he thought he could get her out. He called over to a man nearby. 'Hey, could you help over here? Quickly.'

The man hustled over. They each grabbed an edge of the four-foot long slab of concrete, and on Sam's nod, they heaved it aside, revealing the stricken woman's head below. It was her. It was Yasmin, and Sam recoiled in shock.

'H-hello Sam.'

But Sam couldn't look at her. Yasmin was alive, but he didn't know how. The hand he'd seen was hers, but the arm was no longer attached to her body. The right side of Yasmin's head was caved in by a steel girder. One eye was crushed. Her mouth opened but no more words came. He leaned away and squeezed his eyes shut, a guttural sound following as his heart broke for his friend Malik and his young, pregnant wife. Steeling himself, he turned back to her and looked on as her remaining eye fluttered once, twice, then closed forever.

Malik's young wife Yasmin was dead.

Murdered. On her way to see her own mother.

The baby. Sam willed the man to help him free her from the rubble. There was still a chance the baby could be saved. But no sooner had they heaved the concrete off her completely, Sam knew it was over. Dissecting her midriff was the severed half of an advertising billboard, the white wooden board now covered in blood and...

Sam couldn't bear to look any longer. Yasmin was gone. The baby was gone. She had lost her life. Malik had lost everything.

In an agonising daze of sorrow and his own pain, Sam was helped out of the Underground station by emergency first responders, and into a world he knew would never be the same again. The sunlight blinded his eyes as he was appraised by a paramedic out in Parliament Square, and when satisfied his injuries weren't life threatening, he was shifted along to make room for another injured victim.

He was hustled into a non-emergency ambulance with several others suffering less-severe injuries, and a few minutes later he was being checked into the St. Thomas's Hospital back across the Thames.

Just half an hour after that Sam underwent a series of X-rays to confirm his only injuries were a couple of cracked ribs, and after a nurse had led him to his ward and administered drugs for the pain, Sam drifted off into a deep sleep, in which he dreamt of flaming wreckage and terrorists and bombs and dead, murdered friends.

6

Groggy, and in as much pain as he'd ever known, Sam awoke to the sound of his mobile phone pinging as a text came in. He opened his eyes, and immediately shut them again to protect them from the glare of the harsh hospital lights. He groaned and tried to sit up, the bandages around his broken ribs restricting his movements. He gave up, and eased back down onto his pillow.

A moment later he opened his eyes again, slowly this time, and spotted the TV on in the corner, the sound muted. It was tuned to BBC News. The scrolling headline informed him that two-hundred-and-seventy-three people had been murdered in the attack that morning. A horrifying number.

He had somehow survived. Yasmin had not, he remembered, a stabbing pain suddenly entering his chest. Sam had felt utter devastation when he realised it was her maimed body in the wreckage. Now he felt guilty. He knew he shouldn't. He didn't blow up a busy London tube station. But there it was. Sam wondered if he'd ever get over the guilt.

Jason Collins walked along the bustling, brightly-lit hospital corridor with purpose, passing dozens of doctors and nurses all tending to scores of injured patients. The men, women and children being assessed and treated were the lucky ones. Others hadn't been as fortunate when Westminster Underground station was ripped apart by the blast just a dozen hours ago. But Jason knew Sam was doing okay. He'd checked in with reception on his way up to the emergency ward, and it had been confirmed to him that his friend was indeed one of the lucky ones.

But this wasn't just a social visit. Jason would have to tread carefully.

'Evening, mate. How're you feeling?' he said as he approached Sam's bed.

Sam turned to see his friend. His eyes widened in surprise, then a hint of confusion narrowed them again. With what appeared to be some difficulty, Sam hoisted himself up on his pillows. 'Jason? What're you doing here? How'd you know I was here?'

Jason had expected the question and had his answer ready. He smiled. 'Actually, I didn't know you were here. I'd heard reports of another friend being caught up in the blast,' Jason lied. 'When I came to see her I was horrified to discover you were here, too. I'm so sorry, mate. Terrible luck to be caught up in that mess.'

Jason's well-spoken accent — some would say posh — wasn't fake, but due to the circles he operated within it was often exaggerated. Yet within it was a hard-edged confidence borne out of self-preservation and experience. It was in contrast to Sam's quieter, calmer and definitely more generic Home Counties accent, which had faded over the years as he had settled in central London, where a million alternative accents sounded at once different and the same.

Sam nodded slowly, breathing deeply, then he suddenly winced in agony. Adrenaline had helped mask the pain a little when helping with the survivors, but now he needed more morphine, and he felt the pain in his ribs with each breath.

'Shit, can I call a doctor?'

After a moment Sam's pain eased and he slowly shook his head. 'I'm good. Just need to remember to keep still.' He offered the hint of a smile. 'How's your other friend? Bad injuries?'

'Oh, uh, no... not really. Doctor says she'll be fine. In fact she checked out a while ago, which is why I've come to see you.'

Jason sat down.

'How're you doing?' Sam asked.

For a long moment Jason let his gaze linger on Sam, as if mentally appraising him. A surge of pain made Sam close his eyes momentarily, and he didn't notice Jason staring at him. When he opened them thirty seconds later, Jason broke into a smile.

'Well it looks like you're going to be okay, Sam, eh?'

'Yeah. The doc said that aside from the ribs, a few scratches and a couple of lumps and bumps, I should be fine. They're only keeping me in because of a slight concussion. Must've banged my head in the fall, though I don't remember it.'

Jason nodded, then asked, 'What do you remember?'

To Sam it seemed an unlikely question. A little too forward. He'd just survived an explosion after all, almost certainly caused by terrorists. But it was in Jason's nature to be forward, and he'd never been a shrinking violet, not in anything he did. In that,

Sam knew Jason couldn't have been more different from him, and he let it slide.

'Not too much, to be honest. I was on my way to the office, then I was buying flowers, and then... the noise, the... I'm not sure. Just total madness.' Sam's eyes closed and he grimaced, both in pain and at the images and sounds flashing in his mind. The blood. The flames. The broken bones. The screams. The crumbling of concrete and the twisting of steel. The smell of charred flesh. The...

The sounds of the almost-dead.

Yasmin.

Sam's head lolled back onto his pillow and his eyes screwed tight shut. Yasmin. She had died before his eyes. He hadn't reached her in time. He could've done more, should've moved faster. Sam felt it was his fault she was dead, and above the bed sheets his hands clenched into tight fists.

'Sam? You okay? Can I get the doctor?'

Sam sat up again, his eyes holding back tears. 'No. I'm good.'

Just then two nurses entered the private room. One checked the board hanging on the end of Sam's bed, and made a couple of notes. The other checked the fluid levels in Sam's IV drip. They seemed to linger a little longer than necessary, and Jason fidgeted in his chair.

Sam watched Jason from his bed, a sense of unease coming to him unbidden.

Jason stood and approached the nurses. After muttering something to them so quietly Sam couldn't make it out, they both left the room — and in a hurry, it seemed to Sam. After glancing both ways along the corridor, Jason closed the door behind them. Without saying anything, he returned to his seat next to Sam's bed.

Sam looked towards the door, bemused. Then he let his eyes settle on Jason. 'What was that?'

He didn't say anything.

Sam looked around and realised for the first time he was in a different room than when he'd first arrived. It was fancier. Private. He'd apparently been moved whilst out of it on morphine.

'Why am I in a private room? Why the special treatment?'

Jason didn't respond for what to Sam seemed like an eternity. He simply held Sam's stare, almost as if challenging him to say something. In the end, Sam did.

'What the hell's going on, Jason?'

Jason stood and moved his chair even closer, then sat down again. Now they were only two feet apart. Still, Jason leaned forward and spoke, almost in a whisper. 'Some people are going to want to chat with you, Sam. They want —'

'Wait. Who? What about?' There was a serious tone in Jason's voice that worried Sam.

'They'll want to speak with you about what happened this morning. You were there. Maybe you can help them with their... with the investigation.'

'How can I help them? I was caught up in it like everyone else. Just bad luck. I didn't see anything. How could I have? It was all over in a few seconds. No one could have seen anything.'

The outburst caused a fit of agonised coughing, and Jason stood up, concerned for his friend. But it soon eased, and the pair locked eyes as Sam wiped a trickle of bloody saliva from his chin.

'You're going to be okay,' Jason said. 'Listen, I have to go, but I'll be in touch.'

'Why're you acting so weird? What the hell's going on?'

Sam was suddenly exhausted and didn't have the energy to question Jason any further.

'Just get better, okay? I'll see you soon.' Jason made to leave the room, pausing at the door. He turned to face his friend, his eyes a mix of sympathy and expectation. 'Don't worry about it, okay? Everything's going to be fine.'

And, with that, Jason Collins was gone.

7

A couple of hours later Sam was awoken by the sound of the nurse's trolley wheels squeaking across the tiles in the corridor. He'd been drifting in and out of a fitful sleep since Jason's mysterious visit earlier that evening, and he felt more tired now than he had then. Actually, more tired than he'd ever felt. He was hungry too, and Sam hoped that was why the nurse was there.

'How're you feeling, Mr Barker?' asked the young nurse, whose brown skin reminded him so much in that second of Malik's dead wife Yasmin that he almost recoiled, as if seeing a ghost.

He grimaced, and beneath the sheets his stomach muscles tensed as if expecting a punch, his breath expelling almost like a snort through his nostrils as his teeth gritted. After long moments he finally calmed down. Sweat glistened on Sam's forehead, though he shivered from cold as he stared blankly at the ceiling. 'I... I'm okay. Thanks.'

Harmeet had seen it before. Shock. Classic symptoms, though she thought he'd be fine soon enough. 'I'm glad to hear it,' she said, though for now she wasn't convinced he was at all okay. 'May I offer you some dinner?'

'Yes. Um, yes, please. Listen... I'm sorry.'

'It's okay, Mr Barker. You've been through a traumatic, shocking experience, and you're still experiencing symptoms of shock now. But you're in the right place. I'll be back shortly with some food, okay?'

Sam nodded and closed his eyes. He had never experienced anything like the events of this morning. So much pain. So much suffering. And so many victims. Including his friend's wife. Sam wondered if Malik knew yet. Who would tell him? How could anyone deal with that? Tears threatened once more and he fought to keep them at bay, yet his body now trembled with barely suppressed rage.

Sam wondered what would happen if someone he loved were to die in such terrible circumstances. He wasn't sure he could deal with it. Wasn't sure he could deal with it at all.

Sam thought of his son. What if it was him? What if Benji had been killed? Sam couldn't even imagine. His thoughts turned to Dee. What if it was her who'd been caught up in the atrocity? How would she feel if it was him?

There had been a number of missed calls and frantic texts on his phone, mostly from Benji, Leila and Dee — as well as a couple of work colleagues — and he'd made sure one of the first things he did was to send out a text message to all of them to let them know he was fine and couldn't speak to them right now. They'd have seen the news and would be worried sick.

These thoughts and more were swirling through Sam's addled mind when the nurse returned, wheeling the trolley to his bedside and bringing him back to attention. It had been thirty years since Sam had spent a night in a hospital, after trying a stupid stunt on the new bike he'd been given for Christmas. His failed trick had resulted in a broken tibia and a dislocated shoulder. If his memory served him correctly, the food would be average at best.

But the smells enticing him from the trolley now did not seem average. He sat up, suddenly famished, and was surprised when Harmeet placed the tray in front of him. Sam was amazed to see a bread basket filled with roti and naan. Beside that sat a generous portion of yellow basmati rice. Next to the rice was a bowl of aromatic chicken korma. The tantalising aromas immediately transported Sam to Brick Lane in east London, better known to locals as Curry Street for the quantity of top-notch Asian restaurants and street food vendors lining the road, and once again Sam was reminded that he was in no ordinary public hospital in London. Yet he still had no idea why he'd been moved to a private ward that was way beyond his modest Home Office salary, especially without his permission. Finding out could wait. Filling his protesting empty stomach could not, and he figured even his son would forgive him gorging on the succulent chicken, if just this once.

Sam thanked Harmeet, who excused herself, and he devoured his dinner. There were just a few bites left when something on the wall-mounted TV caught his eye. It was Michael Sullivan, addressing journalists outside the BBC headquarters. The charismatic opposition leader thrived in the limelight, and unlike most of Britain's last few leaders and highly-ranked MPs, he actually possessed the ability to make people listen.

The TV was muted, but Sam read the subtitles scrolling along the bottom of the screen.

'Which is why we, as leaders, should take a stand,' Sullivan said, his eyes stern and his body language strong. 'No longer should we live in fear in our own great cites. No more should we pander to those who would have us weaken our borders and soften our national security. Look where that has got us. First the July seventh bombings in Blair's London in 2005. Our brave and patriotic Queen's guard Lee Rigby, getting slain on the streets in such a barbaric manner. How is it that Sharia Law has become almost commonplace in many Midlands cities? The cowardly concert attack in Manchester in the spring of 2017. And now today? I'm sure I speak on behalf of the Prime Minister and the government, we on the opposition benches and of course the entire nation when I offer my sincere condolences to the victims, and to their families and loved ones. But I'll also add that this must stop. We are a proud nation with an enviable, unmatched history of progression and integration. This is Great Britain. But under previous regimes the Great has been lost. I stand here before you as the man to lead us back into better days, into a brighter future free from fear of enemies both within and beyond our borders. Into a future where we no longer allow the European Union to tell us what to do and how to run our country, whilst we pay for the privilege. Join me on our forward march as I, as leader of my party and the next government, put the Great back into Great Britain.'

Sam flicked off his TV with the remote. There was no doubt about it, the man knew how to speak in public. Sam was a proud Brit too. He had always been staunch in his belief that Britain was indeed great, that his country, a place he loved and whose ideals he believed in with his whole heart, was the greatest country on earth. And despite what had happened, despite how some of those beliefs had been challenged lately, what with a rise in violent crime in London and across the UK, Sam still believed in the institution. How could he not? His country still had the world's best healthcare system. The economy was strong. Its education system was the envy of the world, and had been for two centuries.

Britain was his country. It was his Great Britain, and he could not listen to anyone who said it wasn't.

And as he settled back into the pillows, his belly full of food and his mind full of anger and confusion, he drifted off into a deep sleep.

8

'Thanks for everything,' Sam said to Harmeet as he offered a goodbye to the nurse who'd taken such good care of him.

'Just stay out of trouble, okay?' she replied, adding a cheeky wink for good measure. Harmeet was more used to catering to rich, obnoxious patients in the private ward at St. Thomas's Hospital. Sam Barker had been a pleasant, refreshing and understatedly handsome change. He'd been through something truly awful, but she sensed an inner strength. She knew he'd need it.

The doctors had visited Sam early that morning, and after running a few extra precautionary tests, and after the nurses had re-strapped his chest to help protect his ribs and restrict movement, they confirmed he could leave after lunch. Typically, though, the doctor hadn't got round to actually discharging him until mid-evening.

Even though he didn't live far away at all, there was no way he could walk home from here — at least not for a couple of days — and Jason had offered to come and pick him up. He'd been given some half-decent painkillers, and the nurses had told him the bruising around his ribs would start to reduce soon, which would make it easier for him to walk and get on with things.

He'd spent some of the morning getting out of bed, standing and walking slowly around the room, getting some feeling back into his legs. He braced himself against the windowsill and looked out across the London skyline.

It was another bright and sunny day. It was exactly the same kind of day he'd stepped into yesterday, but a sudden sense of doom clutched at his chest. Sam fought to regain his composure. It was going to be fine, and unless he'd known better it was just another lovely day in London. But Sam did know better. Everything had changed.

For days and weeks after the bombings in 2005, in which several of Sam's colleagues had suffered injuries on their commutes, London had felt different. There was a palpable sense shrouding the city back then that something terrible had happened, and yet Londoners, as they had always done, did not bow down to fear. Instead they rallied together and went about their business. In times of adversity, Sam believed, there was no better place to be than his beloved city. London, and Londoners, had suffered terrible losses during the Blitz in the Second World War. They bounced back. They'd done it again in 2005. They had always done it, and they would do it again now. They were small things which, because of yesterday, now seemed more important.

The simple act of parents walking their kids to school was a massive *fuck you* to the terrorists, as was the sight of commuters jumping straight back on the Underground. Riding the buses. Selling flowers on roadside stalls. And in Underground stations. Just being on the streets. London was changed forever after

2005, yet it was unchanged. Beneath his broken, aching ribs his heart remained filled with pride.

When Jason came to pick him up later that evening, Sam shunned the nurses' offer of a wheelchair, instead preferring to do what he could and regain some of his independence. Besides which, he could walk perfectly well — just not as quickly as he used to, at least for the next couple of days.

They made their way down to the ground floor via the lift, and out into the small car park. Sam managed to clamber into the passenger seat of Jason's SUV — thankful he didn't have to stoop and bend — and put his seatbelt on, wincing as the automatic seatbelt tensioners tightened the belt against his aching ribs.

A few minutes later, they passed under the vast railway lines leading into Waterloo Station, with Lower Marsh opening up on the left-hand side. Jason, however, continued to drive straight on.

'It's a left there,' Sam said, knowing Jason could just swing a left by Lambeth North station and back up Lower Marsh by Waterloo Millennium Green.

Jason didn't reply, but instead turned right at Lambeth North and down the Kennington Road, past the Imperial War Museum.

'Where are you going?' Sam asked.

'Got a little job to do first,' Jason said, his voice neutral.

'What kind of job?'

'Someone wants to talk to you.'

To Sam, this sounded almost like a threat, although he knew Jason had no reason whatsoever to threaten him. It was just his anxieties getting the better of him, he told himself. No need to worry at all.

'Is this what you were talking about in the hospital?'

'Sort of, yeah.'

Jason turned right onto the A3, passed the famous Kennington Oval and turned quickly onto the Brixton Road, the tall car rolling through the corners and making Sam wince in pain.

Despite his questioning, he could see he was getting nowhere with Jason, and he eventually decided to remain silent. If someone wanted to ask him what he'd seen on the Underground — which was nothing — then he'd be happy to tell them that. Right now, he was just happy to be on some pretty decent painkillers and to be sitting relatively comfortably.

And that was what he told himself until Jason pulled the car over somewhere on the outskirts of Dulwich and took a flesh-coloured blindfold and a pair of dark sunglasses out of the glove compartment.

9

Sam was pretty sure he wouldn't be able to find this place again, even if he tried. Jason had told him to put the blindfold on, then the sunglasses over the top. The way he'd looked Sam in the eyes as he told him this gave him the impression he didn't have a say in the matter and that Jason wouldn't ask twice. There was also an implicit tone which said he didn't want to have to be doing this, but it had to be done.

When the car finally stopped and the engine switched off, Jason told Sam he could remove the sunglasses and blindfold.

Sam did so, squinting and blinking as he opened his eyes, expecting the low evening sunlight to be cutting through, but there was almost complete darkness.

'Where are we?' Sam asked, seeing what looked like an underground carpark.

'Further south than you're used to,' Jason replied. 'Come on. This way.'

Sam gingerly stepped out of the car, his breath catching as he tried to reduce the pressure on his ribs, before closing the door behind him. He followed Jason towards a white door at the far end of the small car park, into a waiting area where Jason pressed a button to call a lift.

The lift arrived in seconds, and the pair stepped inside, Sam chuckling inwardly at just how much this seemed like a second-rate movie. Clandestine meetings in secret underground carparks? What happened to the 'open and public' face of the organisation?

'What's this all about, Jason? What's going on?'

'In there,' Jason said, pointing to a door. His tone was firm but friendly, and something told Sam he should trust his friend. In any case, the strong painkillers meant he was close to not giving a damn about anything.

Sam shook his head and let out a small laugh. It really was pathetic. He beamed inwardly as he realised he was quite enjoying this, in a strange way. At any other time his anxiety would be playing merry hell with him, but he had to admit it — those painkillers were bloody marvellous.

The door closed behind him, and Sam quickly realised Jason hadn't come in with him. There was, however, another man in the room.

'Take a seat, Sam,' the voice said, gesturing to an armchair in the middle of the room. 'We got you a comfy one. Heard about the ribs.'

Sam walked over to the chair and sat down. The room was dimmed, but not dark. It had an industrial feel about it, but Sam got the impression that was more natural than forced. There was nothing here that didn't need to be, it seemed, although arguably all of it was strange.

'Why do you exist?' the man asked.

If it was a question meant to intimidate Sam, it would never work. It couldn't. Because ever since he'd first asked it of himself when he was just six years old, he was yet to find a satisfactory answer. Not even close. Sam was far from intimidated at all by that dull question.

The man pointed a small remote control at the ceiling and pressed a button. Gradually, light began to build and spill onto the wall in front of Sam. It took a good few seconds before anything was bright enough or in focus, but by the time he'd begun to make out the shapes and forms, it was obvious this wasn't just any old home movie.

What was going on? Jason hadn't mentioned anything about this. He said someone wanted a chat with him. So why was he being treated like some sort of suspect or interrogation victim?

The tall figure stood just off-centre in front of Sam in that moment. The thirst was drying Sam out from the inside, the horrendous images being projected silently on the wall right in front of him in all their glorious technicolour. They intimidated him. They intimidated Sam no end, to the point that he shrunk away and tried to make himself as small as possible, like a child in a bad dream.

But this wasn't a sleeping nightmare. This was real.

'I'll ask you again, Sam. Why do you exist?' His tone wasn't malicious. If anything, it was kindly, paternal.

Sam didn't really understand the question. He knew what it meant; he just didn't understand why he was being asked it now. Hell, he didn't even know where he was.

'Honestly? I don't know why I exist. Why do you care?'

The man chuckled, but it lacked mirth. 'What makes you think I care? Maybe I don't. But let's just assume for a moment I do. Will you listen very carefully to what I'm going to tell you? *Very* carefully?'

Sam didn't answer that. His mind flickered on what Jason

had said to him at the hospital yesterday afternoon, that someone wanted to speak to him. But who were these people? He glanced up at the wall of alternating images. Explosions flashed silently. Starving children cried. Monsanto protests. Slain elephants. Planes flying into buildings. Politicians. Forests being destroyed. Raging fires. Kim Jung-Il. The twin towers collapsing. Flooded villages. Trump. Lifeless orang-utans. Homeless people. A smirking Tony Blair. The Pentagon. Another politician. Was that the theme here? Politics? Nothing made sense to Sam any more.

'Could I... May I have some water? Please?'

'Of course. How remiss of us,' the man answered. But he wasn't being remiss at all. It was deliberate. 'But first, answer my question.'

Sam figured he had no choice. 'Yes,' was all he said.

'Good,' the man said, before moving closer to Sam.

Sam could see the man more clearly now. He guessed he was in his late fifties, wearing a modest suit. Perhaps five foot ten, and at best of average build. His near-white hair was slightly unkempt, but it sat over a lean yet handsome face. His green eyes, magnified beneath trendy Gucci glasses, were intense. His pleasant face was expressionless, but Sam sensed no hostility there. He relaxed a little.

'Help yourself to the water,' the man said, as a small table was placed next to Sam, complete with large filled jug and a glass. Sam hadn't even noticed the door opening. 'Can I offer you tea?'

'Water's fine,' Sam replied. 'I have a question.'

'Of course. I think you've earned it.'

'Right. Who are you, where am I and what the hell am I doing here?'

The man stared at Sam for long moments, as if deciding whether it was time to reveal what was going on. He smiled and nodded.

'My name is Tom Travers. We are The Firm, and you are at one of our operational bases in London.'

Sam simply stared at the man as if he was joking. The Firm? Was he serious?

Sensing Sam wasn't buying it, the man continued. 'I know how this must look. Very James Bond, no doubt. A little cloak and dagger, perhaps.' His well-spoken, almost lordly English accent only added to Sam's intrigue.

'That's an understatement,' he said, though it wasn't funny.

'The Firm is an internationally recruited group of highly-skilled and dedicated professionals from many specialised fields, who all share one vitally important common goal.'

Sam listened on, incredulity widening his eyes. 'What is this, some kind of joke?' For a moment, he wondered whether this was all a drug-induced hallucination.

'This is far from being a joke, Sam. You promised to listen. May I continue?' The man's voice remained calm, patient, as if he'd given this spiel many times before. Reluctantly, Sam nodded.

'As I said, we share one very important common goal. Our goal is so important, we only recruit to our cause those who share our beliefs and philosophies, those who we believe will help us achieve our ultimate aims.'

Sam could hardly believe what he was hearing. Was this MI5? The man perched on the desk just a couple of feet from him had said they recruited only highly-skilled and dedicated professionals. Did they think he was that?

'And what's that got to do with me? Why am I here?' he asked, a hint of self-deprecating sarcasm in his voice.

'If you haven't guessed it yet, you're here because your personality and specific set of skills has been made clear to us. Call it a recommendation.'

Sam shook his head. He'd never heard such nonsense. And yet... 'My specific skill set?'

'Yes, Sam. You're here because The Firm wants to recruit you.'

10

For the third time in the last five minutes, Abdul Wahid Mohammed peered through his curtains to the street below. He'd been nervously watching the street for hours now, unable to shake the sense that his flat was being watched. Yet he hadn't seen any sign of that, nor any suspicious-looking cars or trucks parked where they shouldn't be.

But his fears weren't without justification. He'd been warned that the authorities were closing in on the splinter cell he'd joined fourteen months earlier, and even though they were months, maybe even years from becoming a serious active unit, things were getting tenser than he could ever have imagined. He sat down on the shabby couch and checked his phone. No messages.

It was mid-afternoon already. He was exhausted, but Abdul couldn't sleep. He hadn't slept properly for weeks now. But it wasn't just a fear of being caught. For a long time now, Abdul had considered how to get out of what he was doing.

In many ways, he still believed in the cause. His issue wasn't with the cause and the philosophy itself, rather it was about the best way in which to achieve it.

Their remit for this splinter cell was simple. Within the first couple of years, his cell was to have carried out several minor bombing attacks on selected targets in west London. Death and destruction weren't necessarily the main goal of the attacks. Other, more well-established and funded cells were responsible for the bigger attacks. Their goals were designed more to keep the public on their toes and to keep the word *terror* on the minds of all Londoners.

But Abdul knew there was no real way out for him. They simply didn't allow it. Deserters were themselves considered infidels, and could no longer be trusted if they quit the cell. If they did leave, then they were as good as dead. Which was why Abdul hadn't just fled. There had to be another way out. He just hadn't yet worked out what it was.

It was only fairly recently that he'd managed to pluck up the courage to approach his closest friend in the cell, Azim al Huq. Azim was a calm and measured person, and Abdul had felt he could confide in him — tell him that he wanted out. Although Azim had responded more like a caring father, Abdul could see in the man's eyes that he had been gravely disappointed. He'd told Abdul he'd see what he could do for him, but Abdul hadn't been convinced. He knew he had to get out before it was too late. But his time was running out.

11

'You want to recruit me? Why? And for what? You haven't even told me what your "great cause" is,' Sam said, raising his hands to produce sarcastic air quotes, emphasising his obvious disbelief. But he immediately regretted that sudden movement when pain seared from his ribs, causing an equally sudden wave of nausea.

Sam took a couple of slow breaths, and looked back at the man standing in front of him, slightly off centre, arms folded. He had to admit there was also something compelling in his expression, even though he could barely make it out through the flickering light of the projector. Whatever this great cause was, it seemed the man before him fully believed in it. Sam backtracked a little.

'Look, I'm sorry. I'm obviously a little stressed right now. I don't know who the hell you are and, let's be honest, I've been brought here against my will. I'm meant to be at home, recovering.'

The man nodded. 'It's okay, Sam. I'm sorry for what happened to you, and I apologise for you not being told in advance what this was all about. But I'm sure you understand we have to maintain a modicum of secrecy in what we do. If you were simply invited here you would have never come of your own volition. And I wouldn't have blamed you. We take what we do very seriously, as you can see, and we have to take every care to remain covert.'

'But why me? What is it you think you know about me? And how?'

The man glanced over into a corner of the room behind Sam and nodded. A moment later, Jason stepped forward.

'Tom and I will answer all your questions, Sam. Okay?'

Sam sat there, hands clasped in his lap and breathing heavily, despite the pain it caused in his ribs. With a sigh of resignation, Sam shook his head and nodded.

'Sam, Tom Travers is my boss. We both sincerely hope he'll soon be your boss too.'

'Boss of what? The Firm? Is that what you called it?'

'Yes, The Firm,' Travers answered. 'We want you to join our ranks.'

'Jason. Yesterday at the hospital you mentioned people wanting to talk to me. Is this what you meant?'

'Yes.' Jason answered.

Sam just shook his head again, finally realising that perhaps Jason's job hadn't been so dull and boring after all. More deep breaths.

'So, are you going to tell me what the cause is? Maybe I'll decide if I think it's great or not.'

Travers and Jason shared a look, and Travers nodded. Jason spoke. 'Look, Sam. We believe that The Firm, and The Firm's cause, is the most important movement happening anywhere on the planet right now. In fact, we're operating all over the globe in dozens of countries. What you see here is only the core of our UK-based operations. And our cause? We have one primary aim, and that is to fight corruption at the highest levels of office. And by office, I mean government. Here in London we're focusing right on our own doorstep. And we want you to help.'

12

Sam's jaw gaped in disbelief. He couldn't even begin to make sense of everything that had happened since he'd left his Waterloo flat for work yesterday morning. There was the bombing. Yasmin's death. All the needless suffering. Jason's awkward behaviour at the hospital. The weird drive here.

In anyone's lifetime, those were some serious events. Each of them should have seemed shocking, yet somehow, and to his complete surprise, Sam didn't feel all that shocked anymore.

But what they were telling him now was the most disturbing of all. He wasn't even convinced he'd heard right. Corruption? At the top reaches of British government? He wasn't naive enough to believe it never happened at lower levels; he'd worked at the Home Office long enough to know it did. He even suspected it occurred at the top of less scrupulous foreign countries.

But corruption that far up in the British government? He'd never heard such outrageous nonsense. And he'd heard plenty. There were always people who claimed the Establishment was corrupt, but he'd like to see them living in North Korea or a war-torn African nation. They didn't know how good they had it.

'You know what? I'm not sure what you think you're really doing, but I do know you're wasting my time. I need to go home. I need to get some sleep. I need to recover from my injuries. I need to visit my friend, whose wife was murdered by terrorists yesterday. And I need you to leave me the hell alone.'

Sam stood again, breathless with pain as he did so, his fists clenched in anger. But he couldn't help it. These people were trying to tell him that the leaders of the best, most democratic and free country in the world, his leaders, of his country, were corrupt. It was time to leave.

'I'm going now. Please show me the way out, and please don't follow me.'

Sam walked towards the door, hobbling as the pain pierced through his ribs. He'd almost reached it when Jason called his name, calm and friendly. Something in his tone told Sam he had to turn back towards his friend. He turned round to look at Jason, but his attention was pulled by the images now being projected on the wall. They were of yesterday's bombing.

From a dozen angles, snippets of video from CCTV cameras showed Sam in horrendous details what had transpired the previous day. There was a scene of the platform, apparently seconds before the blast. People waited patiently for their train. The carriages started to come into view, when suddenly a blinding flash erupted from the rearmost carriage. Flames tore across the platform. Bodies ignited where they stood, burning people alive. Walls crumbled. The ceiling of the platform caved in. Dust and debris swirled through the air, and it reminded Sam of the scenes on 9/11, when the first tower collapsed and dust roared through the streets like a pyroclastic flow. Except this wasn't New York. Nor was it a volcanic eruption. This was a terrorist attack below the streets of London. And he had been caught right in the middle of it.

Seeing the footage like this reminded Sam with stark clarity how lucky he was to be alive. That there were any survivors at all seemed to Sam like a miracle. But he didn't believe in those, and knew it was down to the bravery of the emergency services and anyone else who'd helped — just like he had, or had at least tried to — struggling as he was with his own pain, shock and injuries.

He looked away from the wall of images. He didn't need to be reminded of what happened. He had lived through it. He'd come out the other side. Many hadn't been so fortunate. Sam's arms slumped once more; he hadn't realised he'd been holding them to his face. What the hell was going on?

He turned to see Jason and Travers standing close beside him.

'Sam, listen carefully,' Travers said. 'Yesterday's bombing was not carried out by terrorists. It was what we call a false flag event.'

'Bullshit. You expect me to believe that? And by who? Who would do that? Who would kill all those innocent people?'

Tom glanced at Jason, who continued. 'It's true. The false flag attack was organised and carried out by certain members of the British government, Parliament and Security Services. I can tell you names—'

'Absolute bollocks!' Sam yelled. 'There's no way that's possible. For what reason?'

'It's very simple. Some people think the country is out of control, and will do anything it takes to regain that control. One, in particular. Any guesses?'

Sam just stared blankly ahead, his mind unable to process what Jason was saying.

'How about Michael Sullivan? You know full well he's anti-immigration. Some even say he's an outright racist. One thing that's certain is that he's been advocating for years against what he calls "soft border control" by the government, who he blames for all the terror activity in the last decade or so. It makes perfect sense, if you think about it. And it's not like false flags haven't been carried out before.'

'No. No, Jason. You sound like some brainwashed cult members or deranged conspiracy theorists. Let me go, okay? Now!'

'I can understand why you're upset, Sam. Like I said, we understand. I know it comes as a terrible shock to learn that those people in power, many of them handed it on a plate without democratic justification, many of those men and women charged with protecting our freedom and liberties are in fact the very people taking that freedom and those liberties away. We really want you to stay and recons—'

'Let me go, Jason.' Sam's voice had softened. Fear was taking over. 'Please. I just want to go home.'

'I'm afraid we can't allow you to leave just yet. Like I said, I know you're in shock. But believe me when I say that soon enough you'll come to accept what we're telling you as the undeniable truth. And when you do accept it, you'll willingly join our cause. I'm certain of that.'

Sam had had enough. He was tired of being told what he would or would not believe. 'No, I won't. Let me go.' Sam wasn't a violent man in any way, and he was in no physical state to attack anyone and leave by force. But he really wanted to punch his friend right on his nose.

'Listen, Sam. You need to agree to calm down and reconsider what we're telling you. I think it would be the wisest thing you've ever done.'

Sam didn't appreciate what he considered to be Jason's barely-veiled threat. He'd had enough of this shit. Whatever. He was out of there. 'No, I don't.'

Jason nodded, disappointment in his eyes. 'Then you leave us no choice. I'm really sorry about this, Sam.' He nodded over Sam's shoulder and, before Sam could react, strong arms had clasped his shoulders and he was shepherded out of that room and into the corridor.

13

Trying his best to calm down, Sam focused on his breaths and tried to visualise the reducing pressure in his chest until his breathing slowed to a point that his ribs no longer protested.

He'd been taken to another room, much plusher this time. More comfortable. It was laid out with two leather sofas, a bed, a selection of books and a small kitchenette and bathroom.

They'd told him there was something they needed him to see, but that it wouldn't be ready for another few hours. He'd tried to protest, but they were having none of it.

Why was he here? They had told him why, but it still didn't make any sense. They had definitely got the wrong man.

They had questioned Sam about why he thought he existed, and he hadn't known. Who did? Who knew the answer to that most ancient yet fundamental of existential questions?

Why does anyone exist?

He tried to recall everything they'd told him. Every bizarre thing they told him that he'd never, ever believe. Corruption in the upper echelons of British government? Impossible. Said government committing atrocities against its own civilians? No way.

The Firm? They said their goal was to fight corruption at the highest levels of office. Sam accepted many governments around the world were indeed likely corrupt, and he accepted some members of his own government had probably been corrupted by power or for simple financial gains. But the leaders of that institution? There was just no way. He would not believe that. Showing him those videos of the bombing didn't prove anything. The only thing it proved was that some sick bastards had murdered too many innocent people. Almost including him.

They had said they wanted to recruit him for his personality and special skill set. Was that a joke? Sam was a mid-level IT guy at the Home Office. So what? His specialist area was digital forensics and network security, which he had to admit did give him certain knowledge, or at least access to knowledge that some people might find useful. Was that it? Were they trying to use him to access sensitive government records? And if so, were their claims that they're actually doing good, false? Were they the criminals?

Ultimately, Sam concluded he didn't believe anything they'd told him. Nothing these delusional clowns could show him or tell him could ever swerve Sam from his beliefs that the British government were there only to serve and protect him and sixty-seven million other British civilians. No way. Nothing. Ever.

By now he had no idea what the time was, so when Jason unlocked the door and told Sam to leave the room and follow him, he did as he was told.

It was strange seeing Jason in this place, in this role,

although he was still the same Jason Collins he'd known and been so close to for so many years. That gave him some comfort that everything was going to be fine.

Sam staggered along the corridor, the pain in his ribs fighting against the tiredness in the rest of his body.

Moments later he was in a different room. The men came to a stop, and Sam stood there, unable to believe what he was seeing. Set out before him were perhaps a dozen desks. Each desk had on it what appeared to his exhausted mind to be top of the range high-tech surveillance equipment, with open laptops, monitors and recording devices, and a whole gamut of cables, modems and fancy communications systems. Behind most of the desks sat a studious-looking collection of men and woman of varying ethnicities. On the wall at the front of the room was a series of large flat-screen monitors, each of them displaying different images.

As he looked at the pictures, Tom Travers and Jason entered the room and stood beside him.

'Sorry for the slightly unconventional approach, Sam,' said Travers, 'but we can't take any risks. Besides, there's something we think you should see. Please, come forward, would you? You have my word that you will no longer be manhandled, and when we're done you'll be free to go. That's a promise. But you're going to want to see this.'

14

Many of those people who'd been standing around or sitting behind their desks now approached the vast bank of screens. They congregated just behind Travers, Jason and Sam. In total, a dozen operatives — and, Jason hoped, one future operative — watched on as the screens at first flickered, then cut to what appeared to Sam to be live footage, probably somewhere in London.

'You may remain sceptical about what we've told you until now,' said Travers. 'To be honest, I can hardly blame you. You've had a rough few days.'

'Finally, you've got something right,' said Sam, with barely disguised scorn.

Travers nodded, the hint of a smile curling his lips. 'But what you're about to see, I hope, will provide you with all the evidence you'll need to understand what we do here, and that what we've told you is the truth, as harrowing as it may seem.'

'And what am I seeing here?' Sam asked, his disdain clear. 'Where is this?'

'You're seeing CCTV footage of an address in Balham. We have access to the feed. Do you know Balham?'

'Not well. But yes, I know it.'

'Good. I told you the attack on Westminster Underground station was a false flag. Naturally that's hard to believe. But I assure you it's true. So, if it was a false flag, you're probably wondering both how and why. Right?'

Sam said nothing, but continued looking at the screen.

'Jason, would you continue?' asked Travers.

Jason nodded and turned to his friend. 'Sam, the person who took that bomb onto that train is not the person who's going to take the blame for it. The finer details of that we're looking into, but for now let's assume the guy who's taking the rap for this is not your typical jihadist. Doesn't fit the profile.'

Jason pointed towards one particular screen among the array before them. It showed a still image of a young man who, to Sam, appeared to be of Middle-Eastern descent.

'Meet Abdul Wahid Mohammed,' Jason said. 'A British-born Muslim of Pakistani origin. Abdul is known to both the government and MI5 and, of course, to us, and has been watched for the last twelve or so months, though as yet there's been nothing to get too excited over. The splinter cell he's involved with is only considered to be a Level 2 threat right now, and since the level goes up to ten, he's currently considered a minor player. A trusted contact within MI5 believes that Abdul has aspirations to leave the cell. Apparently a dozen virgins aren't tempting enough.'

There was a muted snickering among the gathered people, but it soon died down.

'So perhaps Abdul is doubting the jihadi cause, which, if true, makes what you're about to see even more pertinent.'

'What am I about to see, Jason?'

'You're about to see the very definition of a patsy.'

15

After yet another failed attempt at sleeping, Abdul Wahid Mohammed clambered out of bed in his dingy flat and relocated to the uncomfortable, threadbare sofa. He'd never been so exhausted in his life, and it was making him ill. He was stressed, too, and his paranoia was growing with every passing sleepless night.

But he couldn't help himself. He parted the curtains and peered out onto the street below. As usual, he saw nothing other than the orange glow of street lamps on an otherwise ordinary road in southwest London.

He hated Balham these days. When he'd first moved south from Leicester after finishing university a couple of years ago, he was excited to be in the big city. He made friends quickly and he loved the mosque he attended on Balham High Road. It had given him the sense of belonging and community he'd lacked since the move south, and he relished it.

But the excitement of being in London soon wore off. His grad course studies at St George's campus of the University of London were dull, and since he'd been approached by the mullah at Balham Mosque he'd felt pressured to become more devout. He'd had many non-Arabic friends at uni in Leicester — many non-Muslim friends. But that was frowned upon down here in this part of the city, and rather than risk being given the cold shoulder by his peers at the mosque, Abdul had played along with their rules.

A year after joining the cell, he now knew it had been the worst mistake of his life. But Abdul didn't know how to get out if it. Every other member of their cell — there were currently six of them — was passionate about the cause, and all were committed to seeing it through to its conclusion, whether that was six months from now, or two years. They were in it until it was finished. But not Abdul. He wanted out, and the stress of it was making him sick.

He peered between the curtains again, and again he saw noth—

Abdul flinched, convinced he'd seen movement along the street, and it was far too late at night, or too early, for that. Over his years living there he'd learned that the last pubs and bars kicked out at one in the morning, and the very latest stragglers were gone by one thirty, two at the latest. Of course there was always the odd person lingering around, usually stumbling along, spilling kebab meat or puke onto the pavement. But it was rare. He strained his eyes.

There. Again, a blur of movement. But it wasn't on the actual street. And it definitely wasn't a car.

Abdul's heart rate ratcheted up a notch, his breaths coming faster. He closed the curtains. He should call Azim.

Azim al Huq was his closest friend in the cell and the man who seemed to know everything that was going on, usually before it happened. But Abdul also knew he had been extra paranoid lately and didn't want to wake up his friend for a false alarm. Still...

He peered through the curtains again, and this time he was sure. Someone was definitely making their way slowly and discreetly towards his flat. He glanced right then, in the other direction from the approaching figure, and now he was certain. Two more shadowy forms emerged into view.

It was as he'd been warned it would be in their early training. If the police or security forces ever raided their homes, it was always in the dead of night and always on foot. It was happening.

Shit, thought Abdul. *This is it.*

He reached for his phone.

EXPECT MORE ATTACKS, SAYS TOP TERROR ADVISOR

Britain should expect to be the victim of more terrorist atrocities, a former special advisor to the Home Office said today.

Professor Lloyd McGowan, who lost his job after speaking out against British-born terrorists being allowed to remain in this country, said people should 'brace themselves for further Islamic terrorist onslaughts' unless politicians took firm and immediate action against those who seek to disrupt British life.

Professor McGowan made his comments in the light of the recent Westminster bombings, when a Muslim terrorist detonated a bomb on the London Underground during the morning rush hour.

London has become an increasingly attractive target for terrorists over the past few years, and it will come as no surprise to anyone that a top expert has now come forward and bravely admitted the truth.

With a general election looming, all eyes are now on the prime minister to see what action will be taken to protect British people from the growing onslaught of Islamic terrorism.

Meanwhile, the leader of the opposition, Michael Sullivan, warned that Britain 'could no longer remain on the back foot' and pledged to increase funding to the security services and counter-terrorism organisations should he become prime minister at the forthcoming election.

The comments by Professor McGowan, who is known to be closely aligned to Sullivan, are likely to be music to the ears of the leader of the opposition.

16

'But if he's not the bomber, why the hell would they be going after him?' Sam asked.

'Because he's the patsy. He's the fall guy. He wanted to leave the cell, but the big bosses weren't having it. Within the next few minutes he'll no longer be a threat to them, and their aims will still have been achieved.'

'What do you mean?'

'Sam, why do you think terrorists are so quickly and easily identified? Don't you find it a bit odd that security services always manage to find the bombers' passports amongst the rubble? A solid metal train carriage — no trace whatsoever. Totally incinerated. But a few sheets of paper somehow, miraculously, manage to survive intact. And who takes their passport to a bombing anyway?'

'You're telling me this is live footage? And that you already know exactly what's going to happen? How? How can you know, unless you're involved?' Sam was frantic.

'Yes, it's live footage, and we know about it because, and you

might not like it or believe this, but we know everything.'
Travers's tone was the epitome of calm, and the man exuded
complete control. It unnerved Sam, but he couldn't take his eyes
from the screen.

'That's good, Sam. Keep watching. What you'll see next is
two separate teams of security forces converging on the flat from
either end of the street. They'll approach on foot, and they'll
stick to the shadows where possible. It's a quiet street and these
officers are well-drilled. They'll get to the stairwell leading up to
the block of flats and will go up those stairs without making a
sound. No one will suspect anything. Not even the chap who's
inside. Not until it's too late, anyway.'

'What're they going to do?' Sam asked

'Those teams — those British security officers — are about to
kill an innocent man.'

Abdul knew it all too clearly now. He called Azim again, and
again he received no reply. He paced around the small lounge,
knuckles clenching and unclenching from the stress. He was
trapped. He couldn't run, because to these scumbags him
running meant that he was already guilty, and by default that
meant he was already a terrorist.

Nor could he wait for them to burst in and then plead his
innocence. There wasn't much in the way of evidence of his
involvement with the cell. But these guys didn't need much.
Abdul had always thought the cell wasn't organised enough.
Not careful enough. This was a low-budget operation at best. At
worst, it was a fucking shambles. They wouldn't even give him a
chance to speak.

And even though Abdul knew he would never have gone through with the cell's plans, never would have hurt an innocent person despite the differences in their beliefs, none of that mattered anymore.

He peered between the curtains again. There they were. Ten, perhaps a dozen heavily-armed anti-terror officers. They were coming. They were going to arrest him. Abdul knew he would spend the rest of his life in prison.

———————

'You have to stop them!' Sam yelled. 'You can't just let them go and kill him. He might not be involved!'

Jason Collins answered. 'That's how this works, Sam, and is what we've been trying to tell you. Whether Abdul Wahid Mohammed is innocent or not, he's been chosen as the face of this particular false flag attack. They know it. We know it. And in...' Jason looked at his watch. '...less than two minutes, Abdul will know it too. They'll arrive at his door. What happens then is inevitable. Nothing will stop them completing this mission, nor would they let it. It's a simple scenario, really. A suspect is chosen. Then a suspect is killed. They will smash through the front door, apprehend the man, take a few photos of him for later use, and...'

'And?' Sam's rapidly-paling face was a mask of incredulous horror.

'And then...' Jason turned back to the screen. The security team had now converged at the communal gate at the front of the property. After a moment's pause, the video showed them streaming two at a time towards the building, where they could be seen rushing up the stairs.

Then they were suddenly out of camera shot, the angle from the nearest streetlamp-mounted CCTV camera too acute.

Jason turned back to face Sam and looked him directly in the eye.

'And then they'll kill him.'

Abdul sat down on the sofa, then stood up again. He didn't know what to do. Azim wasn't answering his calls. Just when he needed him most, his only trusted friend had let him down. The police were less than a minute from his door, which Abdul felt certain meant he was just over a minute from being arrested. So he kneeled. Despite his regrets about joining the cell, and despite the fact he no longer believed in the jihadist philosophy, he was still a devout Muslim.

He would not speak when they came for him. He would not protest. They would find him on his knees in submission, praying to Allah. They probably knew he wasn't armed. Knew he hadn't wired that flat with explosives. Knew he was just another wannabe jihadist with virgins on his mind. That last part wasn't true, and if he wasn't so scared Abdul might have smiled. But he was scared. He was really fucking scared.

His parents back in Leicester didn't know he was in a so-called terror cell. They thought he was at graduate school in London, which, technically, he was, though he'd rarely attended in recent months and now it was the summer holidays. What would they think? Would they believe what they'll say about him, that he was a terrorist?

Yes, he had joined the cell, but he was going to quit. He'd

tried to quit. Abdul's mind raced and swirled with shame and fear and regret.

And on his knees in the shabby flat in Balham, his face pressed to the dirty carpet and his heart pounding in his chest, Abdul Wahid Mohammed prayed. And then he cried.

The officer clutching what was affectionately known as 'The Enforcer' stepped forward and, after receiving a nod from his superior officer, swung the battering ram hard at the cheap wood and glass front door of Abdul Wahid Mohammed's rented flat, which caved in like nothing more than cardboard and plastic. They didn't expect any resistance, nor did they get any. They didn't, however, expect the young grad student to be on his knees in the hallway right in front of the door.

The team swarmed in, and after just three seconds the flat was secured. Two officers hauled Abdul to his feet and stood him upright. Before he could say anything, a bright light flashed in his eyes as someone took a few close-up digital photos.

Tears continued streaming down his face and he knew this was it, that he would be hauled off to prison and dumped in a cell from which he would probably never leave, apart from to appear in court, where he would be declared an enemy of the state, a terrorist, and sentenced to a life behind bars, where shaven-headed prisoners would name him Osama and beat him to within an inch of his life every day until they got bored of him and either left him to rot or put him out of his misery.

That's what he thought was going to happen. But he was wrong.

The officers clutching him pushed him to the ground, and the last thing he saw as he looked up and squinted through stinging tears was the business-end of an automatic weapon, which erupted in a devastating barrage of lethal bullets.

17

From across the Balham High Road, Azim al Huq eased the curtains closed. The sun was just beginning to rise and the anti-terror forces had just discreetly carted away the body of Abdul Walid Mohammed.

Everything had gone according to plan, and after several anonymous tip-offs by Azim himself, the security forces had stormed the flat and taken him out.

Abdul had considered Azim his friend, but as far as al Huq was concerned, he was nothing of the sort.

Abdul had joined the cell a little over a year ago and, while showing early promise, Azim had realised over the last few months that Abdul's heart was no longer in it. Yes, he was a devout Muslim, and yes he still agreed in principle with the overall cause. But Azim was certain that, ultimately, Abdul could not go through with the planned attack. He would let them down, and be a serious risk of exposing the cell Azim had worked so hard to form.

When he'd been contacted a few months ago by Kieran O'Brien with a request for help in an upcoming 'event', he was only too happy to oblige. His task was to recommend two people: someone to actually carry out the Westminster bombing, and someone to set up as a patsy to blame for it.

Azim had been happy to organise both. He had done his part, and the financial rewards would continue to fund further missions, all of which played perfectly into his boss's plans.

The second part of the deal was to supply the patsy. And that had been easy too. In fact, it killed two birds with one stone. It helped his boss, and also removed the weak link in his cell, Abdul Wahid Mohammed.

He pulled out his mobile phone and called Kieran O'Brien.

'Yeah?'

'It's me. Azim. It's done.'

O'Brien didn't say anything, which was normal, and Azim ended the call.

Kieran O'Brien immediately placed a call of his own.

'Kieran.'

'Like clockwork, boss.' There was exactly zero emotion in the Irishman's tone, which was just how Michael Sullivan liked it.

'Excellent work, Kieran, as always.' He paused, and yawned, displaying no more emotion than O'Brien had done. 'We should celebrate. Email Frank. Let's have some fun tonight, eh? Have him organise the girls.'

18

30TH JUNE, 1997. LAN KWAI FONG DISTRICT, HONG KONG.

'Two more doubles, now!' the man demanded, caring nothing for manners. He didn't care. These people didn't deserve them. 'And hurry up.'

The barman's eyes narrowed, but he turned and hustled after the drinks. *Fucking expats*, he thought, and wished every last one of them would get the fuck out of Hong Kong, where they'd been stinking the place up for way too long.

The man collected his drinks without a thank-you and returned to his friend, barely acknowledging the two pretty girls sharing the booth. They meant nothing to him. The women thought they were high-class hookers, but the man saw them as nothing more than toys to be bought, played with and discarded like the trash they were.

He smiled inwardly, recalling the bumper sticker his wife bought for their car: *A Dog is For Life, Not Just For Christmas.* Well, these hookers would be useful for about two hours, then he'd never think of them again.

He grinned at his friend, a stout Northern Irishman he'd met several months ago. It was soon after he had first been posted to Hong Kong to serve as the attaché to Robert Francis Cornish, Foreign Office Spokesman for the Senior Trade Commissioner, Douglas Hurd. They'd formed an unlikely friendship, quickly discovering a shared taste for Hong Kong's dark pleasures — pleasures which came cheap when you worked for the right people in Hong Kong. And none was more useful than the British Government.

Tonight was going to be the party to end all parties. The official handover of Hong Kong back to the Chinese from the British was to take place tomorrow. It was to be a historic day. But that was the thing about history — it was soon forgotten. And the Englishman knew what he was going to do tonight would easily be forgotten, too. Just like the times before.

'Ready to get out of here?' he asked, his voice raised over the throb of shitty nightclub music.

'Aye, let's go,' growled his friend. They stood, and the two girls dutifully followed them, hoping for one huge last payday before many of the Brits left after the handover. There would be more customers. There always would be in one of the seediest cities on the planet. But not everyone paid as well as British politicians and their employees.

Twenty minutes later, the two men and their escorts stepped out of the elevator on the eleventh floor of the Mandarin Oriental Hotel, where they'd checked in using fake names, and entered the Irishman's two-bedroom suite. Sharing a nod and knowing winks, the two men departed into their own rooms, the dutiful whores following them in.

Thirty minutes later, the Englishman returned from the bedroom alone and stepped out onto the balcony of the lounge and lit a cigarette, gazing down at the twinkling lights of Kowloon Harbour below. He'd miss the view. He wouldn't miss the locals. He wasn't surprised his friend was taking longer. The Irishman was more thorough with his preferences and wouldn't return until he'd fulfilled all his desires.

Fifteen minutes later, he grinned as he heard the door click open. The other man came and stood silently next to him, also sparking a cigarette. They stood wordlessly beside each other for many minutes, relaxing after their exertions. Finally, the Englishman spoke.

'I'd better get to the airport. Flight's in three hours.' He turned and looked at his friend. 'Can I leave you to clear up the mess?'

The Irishman smirked. Words weren't his favourite means of communication. He simply nodded. That was enough for the Englishman. He trusted the man to get it done and cover his tracks, and he left with barely another word.

After he'd left, the Irishman made a couple of calls from the hotel's landline, and twenty minutes later a couple of associates arrived to help with the clear up. He knew the girls wouldn't be missed. Just two more nameless hookers in a city full of nameless hookers. He took one last look at the face of the lifeless girl, and marvelled at how easy it was to simply snuff out a life.

He'd had his way — completely against her wishes, after his more physical, less run-of-the-mill preferences ruined her — then had his way again. When she wouldn't stop whimpering, he'd simply put two strong hands around her neck and squeezed until she fell silent. He'd barely broken a sweat. And he felt absolutely nothing. He'd killed hookers before. Probably would again. But now it was time to follow his new friend to London. He'd been promised a job, and he intended to take it up. Besides, there were hookers everywhere. It was time for pastures new.

An hour later the Englishman was checking in at Hong Kong International Airport for his British Airways flight to London Heathrow. He no longer needed to hide behind a false name, so he handed over his maroon British passport to the lady behind the counter. She looked up at the man and smiled, then checked her watch. It was 2:oo am.

'Good morning, Mr Sullivan. I hope you have a pleasant flight.'

19

'We couldn't see the finale, but I can assure you that by now Abdul is dead,' said Travers calmly, as if it was a regular occurrence. 'I guarantee it.'

Sam sat down, unable to look at the screens, even though there was nothing more to see.

'Sam, look at me. Please,' Travers said.

Sam didn't look up. He was fighting hard not to throw up, and felt sick to his stomach about what he'd been told was happening.

'Sam, you need to listen.' It was Jason. 'What you've just witnessed is simply one of dozens of similar events which occur over the course of any given year in modern-day Britain. In your country. Whether you like it or not, it's true, and we, The Firm, are giving you a chance to help stop it. Will you join us, Sam?'

Finally, after his nausea passed, Sam stood up. His face was pale, and even though he couldn't see himself, if how he felt was anything to go by he knew he looked like shit. But he was not having this. Not having any of it.

He approached Travers and stood right in front of him, their faces just inches apart. He stared at the man, willing him to reveal it was all a joke, all a big mistake. But Travers stood there, unmoved, barely even blinking.

Sam turned to Jason, the man he'd known for over thirty years and a man who was someone he trusted. Surely he could help Sam make sense of all this, help him understand what this was, why he was even there and why that man had to die?

But Jason was equally unmoved and unflinching. This was not a joke. It was all deadly serious.

'Go home, Sam,' Jason said. 'Get some rest. God knows you deserve it, and by the looks of it, you need it. So go. But when you wake up tomorrow and turn on your television or radio, I'm certain of what you'll see or hear.'

Sam just stared at Jason, exhaustion threatening to overwhelm him. He couldn't speak. Didn't have the energy to argue. He almost wanted to cry, but he would fight that urge until the end in front of these cold, callous bastards.

Jason continued. 'You will hear that a young Muslim man by the name of Abdul Wahid Mohammed, a well-known Islamist with ties to several highly-political preachers in the west London and Leicester areas, and known to be the Westminster bomber, was apprehended at his flat in Balham in the early hours of this morning. You will also hear that, as he was taken into custody, Mohammed somehow managed to break free from his captors and then managed to commit suicide. That's what you will see on all the news channels tomorrow morning. It's what the headlines on all the papers will read, and that's what you'll hear on every news radio station from here to New York. It'll be hailed as a victory for the intelligence community, and a huge step forward towards making Britain safe again for the British. That is what you will see and read and hear, Sam. I promise you. And when you hear it, remember that it is exactly as we told you it would be.'

Sam continued staring at Jason Collins. He couldn't take this anymore, and he couldn't — wouldn't — believe it. It couldn't be true. His government could not do that. They just wouldn't. But even before that stream of thought had passed, an element of doubt had begun seeping into his mind.

'Go home,' Travers said. 'But I know you'll be here again.' Travers turned and walked away, disappearing through a door without looking back.

'Come on. I'll take you home.' Jason placed a gentle hand on his friend's shoulder and led him through a couple of doors, then down a long, dimly-lit corridor. After a couple of turns they came to an internal parking bay.

'This one,' Jason said, signalling towards his car. 'And for your own safety, you'll need to wear this again. Sorry.' Jason held out a blindfold and a pair of sunglasses.

Sam narrowed his eyes, once more in disbelief. But he had no plans to agree to all this, and understood that if he knew their location and didn't come on board, he could compromise every-thing. And that would likely be dangerous to his health. He snatched the items from Jason and climbed into the car, putting them on without speaking.

Jason eased the car out of the underground carpark, turning out onto a deserted industrial estate which, unbeknown to Sam, was on the outskirts of Crystal Palace in south London.

They didn't speak as Jason sped north towards Waterloo, and no words had passed between them when, nearly half an hour later, Jason pulled the car to a stop right outside Sam's flat.

'You can take that off now. Sorry about that, but... Well, you know.'

Sam took it off and squinted as his eyes adjusted.

'Get some rest, mate. You're going to need it,' Jason said.

'Mate? Is that a joke?'

'No. Not a joke. Listen, just don't forget to tune in to the news when you wake up, eh? You know what you're going to see.'

Both mentally and physically drained, Sam turned to face Jason. He looked at him for long moments, then eased out of the car, his ribs pleading for mercy. With the last of his depleted energy, he unlocked the door, relieved it was too early for Emma's bike to get in his way. He trudged up the stairs and, thirty seconds later, still fully-clothed and unwashed, and after swallowing four ibuprofen, Sam collapsed into his bed. He was asleep in seconds.

20

Sam's phone rang, startling him half to death. It wasn't really that loud, but it certainly sounded that way in his mind-numbingly exhausted state.

He rolled over to grab the phone from the bedside table, but it stopped ringing. Squinting open one eye, he could see full daylight streaming in through the flat's windows.

Sam groaned and rolled over. Then his eyes shot open. Only a carefully selected bunch of people had his mobile number. And none of them would call at 5.47 in the morning. 5.47?

But then in a moment of clarity he knew who it was. Not Dee. Not his office. Not his mother. She never called, unless it was his birthday or if someone in his family had died. As far as he knew, neither was true.

It was The Firm. Probably Jason. Sam groaned again, then swung his legs from the bed and staggered to the bathroom. Glancing at himself in the mirror, he saw his pupils were hugely dilated. Next, and almost on autopilot, he made his way to the modest living room and turned on the television. He didn't want to. The Firm had told him to, or at least suggested he listen to the radio. He had sworn to himself when he left the warehouse that he wouldn't do it, would not seek out the news. But he couldn't help himself. He was drawn to the TV as if it was a siren, beckoning him to his imminent demise.

And, as he sat back on the sofa in his tiny lounge, the bright summer sun streaming through his dusty venetian blinds, he already knew what he'd see.

The BBC reporter stood on the pavement outside a block of flats, her weary features serious as she spoke live to the camera.

'The suspect, named as twenty-five-year-old Abdul Wahid Mohammed of flat number sixteen, Balham Rise, which you can see just behind me here off the Balham High Road, was pronounced dead in the early hours of this morning by the Greater Metropolitan Police after what we've been told was an armed standoff. Unfortunate, they say, because Mr Mohammed was believed by the Security Services to be the Westminster bomber, and of course now he will not be able to face justice. The details of Mr Mohammed's death aren't clear to us yet, but we're hearing early reports that it might have been suicide. Mr Mohammed had been arrested during the anti-terror raid earlier this morning at his flat here in Balham, in what police are declaring a successful step towards ridding Britain of Islamic terrorism. There's still a long way to go, they added, but declared they would not be beaten in the ongoing battle against domestic terror.'

The camera panned away from the reporter and zoomed in towards Abdul's flat, where two officers stood either side of where Abdul's front door once was.

Sam closed his eyes, though they were almost closing by themselves. He had never felt so tired. Then again, he had never been put through the wringer quite like he had in the past couple of days.

He felt sorry for himself. He hated that feeling, but felt powerless to stop it. Hundreds of people had died brutal, violent deaths in the bombing of Westminster, yet he had survived. He was lucky. But as he sat slumped on his sofa in the near-dark of a Wednesday morning, he did not feel lucky at all.

Sam peeled himself off the couch, wincing in agony as his ribs reminded him they were still broken, and somehow made it to the bathroom. After relieving himself, he decided to go back to bed, though he doubted there was any point. Despite the addled state of his mind it nevertheless swirled with images of Yasmin and the burning wreckage, of countless victims; many of them faceless, others his own. Some of them Benji. When the images of the bombing faded, words replaced them. *False flag. Corrupt governments. We want to recruit you.*

Sam gave up after ten minutes and staggered in a blur back to the bathroom. He tried to block it all out. He had a job. Some people would call it an important job. His injuries weren't bad enough to prevent him sitting at a desk, and Sam figured he had to turn up. Besides, he didn't know what the point of sitting around at home would be. He'd just be stuck there thinking about everything that had happened with The Firm. Going to work seemed the logical — and the most normal — thing he could do.

He stood under a hot shower for ten minutes, then dressed and made his way down the narrow stairs to his boxy kitchen. He filled the kettle; it was at least a two-cup morning. Probably three. And then he spotted the note.

Pinned beneath a cheesy fridge magnet of a Beefeater, the

fuzzy-hatted Queen's guard, was a note. Its scrawled words were simple:

The Barley Mow, 1pm.
When you change your mind.
Ask for a 'London Pride'.

Sam could count on one hand the people who knew where he lived, and one of them was his landlady. It was more or less the same few people who knew his mobile number. Benji and Leila. Malik from downstairs, and his wife, Yasmin. His dead wife Yasmin. His mother didn't know his address. At least, she'd never sent him a card on his birthday. Of course, his girlfriend Dee knew his address. And Jason. But that was about it.

Sam sat down at the small table and put his head in his hands. He screwed his eyes shut, hoping everything would go away but knowing it wouldn't. His breaths came heavily now, his throbbing ribs a reminder he'd been in a near-fatal bombing. He felt strange. His heart pounded to the point of palpitations, and for a second he feared he was suffering a heart attack. But after a moment it passed. His skin was cool and clammy. He grabbed some cold water from the fridge and downed a whole glass, quickly followed by another. Sam knew he was still experiencing symptoms of shock.

After a few minutes of sitting in the cool, dark kitchen and drinking as much of the cold water as he could manage, Sam felt a little better. He flicked the kettle back on. He thought again about the few people who knew he lived here in his poky flat in Waterloo. Malik and Yasmin. Two of the nicest people he'd ever met. Emma, his slightly scatty, slightly batty landlady. They had clashed occasionally, usually about the pain-in-his-arse bike she left in his doorway. But otherwise he knew she was a nice lady, and the only bad thing she'd ever done that Sam knew of was docking Malik an hour's pay for being quarter of an hour late during a tube strike.

Sam couldn't even believe he was thinking of these people as if they were on a shortlist of break-in suspects. But he couldn't help it. He was well and truly rattled by recent events, and his shredded nerves were wreaking havoc with his rationality. But there it was. It wasn't his fault. Anyway, neither Emma nor Malik nor Yasmin had a malicious bone in their bodies.

Which, other than Jason — who had to be the most likely suspect — left only Dee.

As soon as he thought it, Sam felt ashamed of himself. They'd been friends, colleagues and then lovers for the last three years and Sam was certain he knew almost everything about the lively redhead from Wales. Like in the worst kind of movie, they'd met on a work Christmas party in 2016 and, despite being at opposite ends of the introvert-extrovert spectrum — Sam being as introverted as anyone he knew — they'd hit it off. Sam almost smiled. He had always considered Dee several grades above his station in the attractiveness stakes, and was surprised she'd stuck with him as long as she had.

But someone had been in his flat, and he had to assume it was someone from The Firm. That meant Jason had passed on his home address, knowing someone would use it to break in and intimidate him. And that was not okay. He was done with their threats. He would go to their meeting. But it was not because he had changed his mind. Far from it.

21

In a daze, Sam descended the stairs and left his flat. There was no bike to contend with. Out of respect for Malik and Yasmin, Emma had apparently — and wisely — opted to close the café and the bookshop for the rest of the week, despite the dent it would make to her income, particularly during the busy summer rush.

Sam had called the office to say he'd be a little late, and took a slow walk towards his work at the Home Office building, located just across the Thames on Marsham Street. He went a different way today; he didn't need to see the devastation at Westminster Underground station any time soon. His usual twenty-minute walk took more than an hour, and when he stepped out of the lift at the floor where his office was situated, the first person he saw was Lucy. She jogged over and wordlessly wrapped him in a tight hug. Lucy would never know she was the reason he was caught up in the bombing at Westminster, because he would never tell her.

'Ow,' he teased. 'Mind the ribs.'

'Oh shit, sorry,' Lucy said, and loosened her grip a little.

'Sorry I didn't get you a present. I mean, I did, but I forgot to bring it.'

'I'll forgive you this time,' she said, smiling. 'I'm so glad you're okay. I was worried about you. We all were.'

Sam doubted that second part, but he knew Lucy had been worried sick when she learned he was caught up in the bombing.

'Shouldn't you be at home recovering?'

'Probably. But who's going to stop the Russians hacking all our precious data? Look, I'm fine. Really. Just going to take it easy for a while. But thanks for worrying.'

'Anything I can do?' Lucy asked.

'I'd love a coffee.'

'Coming right up.'

'Um, I haven't had any breakfast...'

'Don't push it, Barker,' Lucy said, smiling, and she turned, walking away towards the staff café. Over her shoulder, she called out, 'Bagel, with the works?'

An hour later, Sam was almost asleep at his desk. He couldn't focus on any of his tasks, and the pain from his ribs was exhausting, despite the heavy-duty painkillers he'd been prescribed by the hospital doctors.

He knew he should have stayed at home and hidden away from the world for a month. But it wasn't only the tiredness and pain affecting his concentration. It was a hundred other things, not least his fast-approaching meeting with The Firm. It was simple. He was going to go to the pub they'd suggested, The Barley Mow, at the arranged time, and he was going to tell them they were out of their minds if they thought they could convince

him that the government was capable of such sickening atrocities. The government he worked for, his employer, whose offices
he was in right now? He knew that people in positions of wealth
and power would — and could — abuse that, but for a British
government to sanction or orchestrate an attack on its own
citizens?

Despite his steadfast conviction that none of what Jason and
Travers had told him could be true, Sam couldn't help glancing
about his office at his colleagues, some of whom he just about
considered acquaintances. If what they'd inferred was true, then
were some of the people he could see from his desk right now
involved? It was ridiculous. Of course they weren't, and he
smiled at the thought of grumpy old spinster Janet Barlow in
accounts colluding with spies and trading sensitive state secrets.
But it really wasn't funny. It wasn't funny at all.

Quarter past twelve came around, and Sam had done
precisely no work since he'd arrived, which was still more than
he believed most of his colleagues had done. At least he had an
excuse. A good one. He left the office feeling strangely buoyant.
He was going to tell whoever was there to meet him at the pub
that he straight up wasn't interested, and to leave him the hell
alone.

At least, that's what he thought was going to happen as he
strode purposefully towards The Barley Mow.

22

Sam glanced at his watch. He was early. There weren't many things Sam hated, but tardiness was one of them. He saw the Barley Mow pub ahead of him along the Horseferry Road. He hadn't felt nervous until now, but suddenly he was questioning why he was even going. He didn't need to go. He could just ignore what had happened and get on with his life. But would they leave him alone? Would The Firm, whoever they really were, just let it go? Even if there was some truth in what they'd said, Sam wasn't the enemy. If they were supposedly the good guys, they surely wouldn't punish him just because he didn't trust them.

And it was Sam's trust that kept him moving towards the pub and towards his meeting with The Firm. His trust in his own instincts. The trust and faith he had in his government. His trust that whoever was responsible for the bombing would be brought to justice, whether he was involved or not.

He swung open the door to the Barley Mow and stepped inside. Then he stopped dead in his tracks.

Sitting at a booth tucked in the far back corner of the pub

was Dee. But his girlfriend was supposed to be in north Wales visiting family, which was why she hadn't been able to visit him in the hospital.

Dee spotted Sam enter the pub. She took a deep breath, smiled, and stood to greet him.

'Dee, what are you doing here?' he asked as she approached, but even as he said it a knot formed in his gut.

'Hi. Can I get you a drink?' Dee usually hugged Sam when they met up. Today she didn't.

'But why are you here? I thought you were... You're supposed to be in Snowdonia.'

'I am. I was. Sort of. How about a drink? A pint?'

'I... No, sorry, I'm... I'm meeting someone.'

Dee nodded. 'I know you are. A pint, Sam?'

Sam's knees suddenly felt weak. He felt dizzy too, as if he'd been drugged. Dee grabbed his arm and led him to her booth.

'Take a seat, Sam, and I'll get you a pint. London Pride, was it?'

Sam sat in the booth, physically recovered but mentally destroyed. 'You've been lying to me all this time? About everything?'

'No Sam, not everything. But you're right, I have been hiding certain things from you. I'm sorry, really I am. But it was very important. Very, Sam. You have to understand that.'

Dee's feelings for Sam were real. She'd fallen in love with Sam in the first few months they were dating, and only recently had she forced herself to back off just a little bit. She didn't want to. It was an order from The Firm. Since The Firm had first started to consider Sam as a recruit, they'd insisted she continue her relationship with him as if nothing was different. But now her boss Tom Travers was convinced of Sam's credentials and obvious value to the cause, his tune had changed and he'd informed her in no uncertain terms that her relationship with Sam could go no further because it would undermine her integrity. Despite her protestations it would do no such thing, she'd relented. The cause was more important than her happiness. That was just the simple truth of it. If Sam were to join The Firm, they were going to have to part ways. She hated it, but her duty was to The Firm and to her country. She only hoped Sam would understand.

Since Sam had become of interest to The Firm, Dee had been monitoring his life closely, and not just during the times they'd been together outside of work. He didn't have many other friends, so that had been fairly easy to manage, especially since two of his few friends were her and Jason Collins. They'd bugged his landline at the flat, but sadly no one ever called it. They listened in on every call made to and from his mobile, but again, eighty percent of those involved his son and Dee herself. He'd been the easiest potential recruit they'd ever monitored.

They were analysing Sam's character. For anyone to get recruited into The Firm, Travers had to be certain beyond any doubt about the strength of their personality and the depth of their integrity. They could have no religious bias. No religion at all, because religion clouded judgment. There could be no skeletons in their closet, however far in the past they were, or however distant. And they could have no family concerns. Sam had a son, but The Firm didn't consider that to be a problem. If anything, it could be an asset.

Dee felt bad for Sam. But her primary concerns were not Sam's feelings, nor the feelings of others like him. Her job, and

The Firm's mission statement, was to protect the citizens of the world from their own governments. And Dee knew with her whole heart Sam Barker would make an excellent recruit for The Firm to meet those objectives.

Sam being caught up in the Westminster bombing had given them the perfect opportunity. If The Firm knew anything, they knew that when opportunity knocked, however terrible the circumstances, you took it.

'Sam, listen to me. The work we do is crucial to the millions of people in this country who don't know the truth. The same goes for our units around the world. Billions of people, Sam. Billions are being lied to in countries on every continent by corrupt, power-hungry, greedy governments. It's been happening for centuries. It's happening right here, right now, in this city. Our city.'

Sam was listening but the words didn't make sense, not least because it was Dee saying them. His mind was a blur and nothing she said sounded right, almost as if it was a foreign language and he only understood every second or third word. Dee continued.

'Your city, Sam. The government that we are currently living under is lying to us. To you. To our families.'

Sam looked at Dee then. 'Families? You leave Benji out of this.'

'Look, my point is that we are trying to protect innocent people from threats they don't even know about. If nobody does anything, the future's going to look very bleak. We're already having our civil liberties taken from us. And it's not even that bad in Britain. Many countries have it a lot worse than we do. That's why we have units all over the world. Anywhere governments rule their people with lies and deceit, sometimes force, we're there on the ground trying to make a difference. And we need good people working with us to make the biggest difference we can. Good people, Sam. People like you.'

'Like me? That's what Jason said. I assume you two are working together, spying on me and sharing my secrets?' He shook his head in disbelief.

'You don't have any secrets, Sam. Not bad ones, anyway.' Dee smiled, but Sam ignored her. 'Jason and I share the same goals. As does Travers. We all do.'

'I thought it would be Jason here today. He send you to do his dirty work?'

'It's not dirty work. I can't stress how important what we do is. And no, he didn't send me. We've been watching you for a long time.'

'And where's Jason now?'

Dee nodded to another corner of the pub.

Sam followed her gaze, and saw a man reading a newspaper. He closed his eyes and breathed deeply. This couldn't be happening.

'But why me?' Sam finally asked. 'What are these so-called skills you apparently need so much?'

Jason folded away his newspaper, walked across the pub and took a seat opposite Sam in the booth.

'I understand what you must be thinking right now, mate, but —'

'Don't "mate" me. And you have no idea what I'm thinking right now!' he replied, realising he'd raised his voice a little too much.

Jason grimaced and looked around. No one seemed to have paid them any attention, but they could never be too careful.

'Okay, you're right,' Jason said. 'Please, just hear us out.'

Sam breathed out through his nose, his jaw clamped shut to stop himself saying what he really thought.

'Listen, before we tell you why we need you in particular, let me tell you a little about what happened with the bombing and the raid on Abdul Wahid Mohammed. We told you it was a false flag. You were sceptical. But —'

'Sceptical?' Sam almost laughed, but things were becoming less comical by the minute. 'Sceptical doesn't quite cut it, Jason. 'I'd say it was bullshit.'

Jason nodded, a hint of a smile creasing his eyes. 'Well, it was a false flag. A classic, in fact. As for the capture and apparent suicide of Abdul Wahid Mohammed, well, we told you exactly what would happen, didn't we? Right down to the minutest of details. How would we have known all that, unless we did actually know?'

Sam stared at Jason. He hated to admit it, but Jason and Travers had told him exactly what would happen. They'd told him Mohammed would die, even before the team had entered the man's flat. They'd also told him it would be all over the news within a couple of hours of the event.

'I saw on the news that the Muqatili Alhuriyati terrorist group has claimed responsibility for the bombings,' Sam said. 'I know full well they've been responsible for several terrorist acts over the last few years. How do you explain that? If it was them, how could it've been a false flag? Why would they admit responsibility if they didn't do it? It's absolute bollocks, Jason.'

The Muqatili Alhuriyati group had risen to infamy and unfortunate prominence over the past five or six years, having carried out numerous bombings and suicide attacks on cities across Europe and the western world. From the van attack on a Copenhagen junior school to the bombings of the Christmas markets in Prague only a few months previous, there was absolutely no doubt that Muqatili Alhuriyati were one of the biggest terrorist threats in the world right now. They had no reason at all to claim responsibility for an attack that wasn't theirs.

He turned his gaze on Dee. 'And how the hell have you been caught up in all this? It's —'

'Sam, could you please keep your voice down a little?' Dee's features were soft, and she understood Sam's reticence. She had been in the exact same position as Sam several years ago when Travers had recruited her. She hadn't believed any of it then either. But that was then. She'd been shown things, evidence of what went on behind the government's facade, things that had shocked her to her core. She wanted to make a difference. She had to. She hoped Sam would soon be fighting against those corrupt bastards alongside her.

Sam nodded an apology. 'Okay, but how can you explain that to me?'

Jason continued. 'Before we get into that, let me tell you why The Firm wants you on board. Firstly, it's your character. You're one of the rare people on this planet who simply cannot be tainted by selfishness. You are, to put it bluntly, squeaky clean. Never had a parking ticket. Never been caught speeding, not because you were lucky, but because you've probably never sped. You leave parties early. You've never been late for work, not once. Except this morning, of course.' Jason smiled and, despite himself, Sam almost smiled too. Almost. 'Listen, quite frankly, Sam, you're boring, which is totally meant as a compliment, believe me.'

'That's a compliment? Thank god you're not abusing me, eh? Not sure I could take it,' he said, shaking his head again. 'And what about this alleged skill set I keep hearing about? This should be fun at least.'

Dee took over. 'You won't like this, but I've been monitoring your work for the last two years. I know everything you've ever done at the Home Office. Everything. And, of course, I've shared your phenomenal work records with The Firm. Quite honestly, you're brilliant at what you do. And you do it not because you're asked to, but because you care. You're helping so many people, probably without even knowing it. And that's not all.'

'Of course. Why would I think that was it, eh? Today's just full of surprises, isn't it?' Sam's tone dripped with sarcasm, but he could feel his resolve starting to slip. These guys knew so much. About him. About his work. His family. Apparently, and they said it themselves, they knew everything. It was terrifying.

'Think about it, mate,' Jason said, though he doubted Sam considered him much of a mate any more. 'With your skills, and your strategically crucial job and the access it could provide you to, let's say, certain sensitive data streams... Think about all the good you could do.'

'You're asking me to, what, spy on my own government? That's treason.' Sam's brow furrowed in disbelief. 'Are you completely mad? I mean, you're here bleating on about terrorists and false flags and who knows what else, and you want me to spy? On my own government? And you're telling me they're the bad guys?' Sam stood up, knocking against the table and spilling Dee's untouched drink onto the floor. 'I'm out of here. You two have lost your minds. Just leave me alone, okay? I want nothing to do with you.' He stared at Dee then. 'With either of you.'

Jason stood up too, as did Dee, who placed her hand on Sam's arm. They looked around, and it appeared no one had noticed the disturbance. 'Calm down, Sam. Please, sit down and let us convince you.' She wasn't sure Sam would ever trust her now. He obviously, and quite rightly, felt she'd betrayed his love and trust. In a way she had, but she would have to live with that. 'Give me just one more minute, and you can ask any questions you want. Okay?'

Sam stared at Dee and Jason with such disdain that for a second Jason thought he might even take a swing at him. But he knew that wasn't Sam's style. Never had been. He was passionate, but passive. Some might even say cold. That was good. He could be calm under pressure. A good quality for a new asset.

Sam sat down, hands shaking through a mix of stress and anger. 'One minute,' he said. 'Then I'm gone.'

'Okay. The floor's yours. Ask any questions you want.' Jason spread his palms out in front of him, as if to say go for it.

'Okay, how about this one.' Sam's eyes were wide, his mouth curled in a smirk, as if he knew they couldn't possibly give him a satisfactory answer. 'You say the Westminster bombing was a false flag? Then how do you explain away all the atrocities carried out by the Muqatili Alhuriyati group? No one's ever questioned those claims before, so why are you now? Explain that, Collins,' Sam said, ignoring Jason's first name. The time for pleasantries was over.

'You're right. No one's ever questioned Muqatili Alhuriyati's claims that they carried out all those attacks and killed all those innocent people. But that's just the thing, Sam. There's one very good reason for that.'

Sam stared at Jason. 'Oh yeah? What?'

Jason narrowed his eyes and looked back at Sam.

'They don't exist.'

24

Not for the first time in recent days, Sam didn't know whether to laugh, cry or run.

How the hell could Muqatili Alhuriyati not exist? Almost every leading news story in the past year had been about them.

'You've got to be joking,' Sam said, his mouth smiling, but his eyes showing something very different.

'I wish I was,' Jason said. Sam had known him for many years, and there was something in his friend's eyes which told him he was deadly serious.

'But they've claimed responsibility for god knows how many attacks. They've been quoted in the news. You can't just tell me all those attacks we're made up.'

'No, of course not. The attacks happened. But Muqatili Alhuriyati weren't responsible. Not in the way you might think, I mean. There's a lot more to it than that.'

'Like what?'

Jason sighed. 'That's the bit we're struggling with. We have our suspicions, but that's not good enough. There's too much at stake. We need hard evidence. Something incontrovertible.'

Sam shook his head. 'I seriously have no idea what you're talking about, Jason. This is crazy.'

'Listen. All terrorist organisations have some sort of footprint. We can trace the members, find financial links, follow leads. Look at some of the other groups that've been in the news over the years. The Taliban. Al Qaeda. There were footprints. We knew some of them had links to the Saudi government and to other states we were on friendly terms with. That's when it became political and diplomatic; the government couldn't sever our ties with those countries, even though they were funding threats to our democracy. It's all about money. But this is something else. Muqatili Alhuriyati have no footprint. To this day, we've still not been able to trace a single member of the group.'

'That just means they're good at what they do, surely?'

'No. It means they don't exist. Tracing members of organisations isn't difficult. Not in the slightest. Working out how they all piece together, who the organisers are, where the chain of command goes — that's where the real work comes in. For a group of those purported capabilities, and who've managed to conduct as many attacks as they have, we'd expect to have two or three dozen members or contacts in our sights. Muqatili Alhuriyati don't fit any of the conventional patterns.'

'So they've got a new way of doing things. And what?'

Jason shook his head. 'No way. You can't just remain invisible. These guys are ghosts. And ghosts don't exist. Therefore neither do Muqatili Alhuriyati. Our contacts in Pakistan have never met a single member of the group, despite having come across plenty from much smaller organisations. We've been studying these sorts of groups for years, and I can tell you nothing feels right.'

Sam sat silently for a moment. 'So you want me to believe

that one of the biggest threats to our democracy doesn't exist, purely because you've got a gut feeling?'

'No, Sam. The biggest threat to our democracy exists alright. There's no doubt about that. But Muqatili Alhuriyati is a front. It's a convenient cover for what we think is really going on. And as for gut feeling, my gut is rarely wrong. You know that.'

'And that's meant to be good enough?'

'Sam, you're an investigator. If we had all the evidence and knowledge to hand already, you wouldn't even be involved. We'd have dealt with it by now. Your job is to find that evidence, to uncover the missing links. All we can do is give you our suspicions or tell you where we want you to look. It's not up to us to provide you with the evidence. Quite the opposite. We're not asking you to give up your loyalty to your country. If you're so sure we're wrong, this is your opportunity to prove it. Use your skills to prove that your unswerving loyalty isn't misplaced.'

Sam sighed. 'Mate, I've known you a long time. But this is madness. You can't be serious.'

Jason looked Sam in the eye. 'You can lead a horse to water, but you can't make it drink. Ball's in your court, Sam.'

25

Sam's answer to Dee's question was categorical. She'd asked him again if he would join The Firm, and again he'd said no.

Dee really thought they'd got through to Sam. She knew how patriotic and loyal he was to his country. But she'd thought that ultimately that would play into their hands. Once Sam realised how betrayed he'd been for all these years, why wouldn't he want to fight back?

But it was Sam's loyalty and patriotism now that was holding him back, preventing him from grasping the enormity of the situation, and blinding him to what Dee and Jason knew was the clear and obvious truth; that the leaders of his government had been lying to him. To all of them.

Nevertheless, his denial was strong. 'I don't believe what you're saying. It's as simple as that. I'm not calling you two liars. But I think you're wrong. Deluded, perhaps. Whoever's feeding you this shit is wrong. Is it that Travers bloke? If you're willing to act against the British government, then you're the ones who should be on trial, not them. You're no better than the terrorists, committing acts of treachery against your own people. I can't believe it's true. I won't believe it.'

Sam wanted to be shocked to his very core by all of this. Wanted to laugh at them and call them lunatics. They were basically telling him that everything he'd ever believed was a lie. That his fundamental belief his government was there to serve him and people like him was a lie. Not only that, but two of only a handful of people he trusted were part of that lie. He wanted it all to be one big joke. But something niggled. Something flickered at the edge of his conscience.

Sam didn't know where to turn, and he suddenly felt as lost and alone as he'd ever known. He grabbed his untouched pint and slumped back against his seat. He took a deep breath and slugged down half the beer in one go, his eyes closed tight.

Jason and Dee glanced at each other. It wasn't over.

'Think about all the good you could do,' Dee said. 'Think about what sort of world the kids of today are growing up in. Including Benji.'

Sam's eyes opened, but he didn't speak, his pale face wearing a haunted look.

'She's right,' Jason added. 'You're being given a unique opportunity to do something amazingly positive with your life. Something that can help shape the future of this country for your boy, and for millions of other kids. For too long now our government and others like them have been getting away with everything. Collusion with rogue states, illegal wars on foreign soil, the murders of innocent people. We can do something about that. You can do something about that. You just need to understand, that's all. Why don't you look into it and find the evidence to prove me wrong?'

Sam wanted desperately to deny it all, to call Jason a liar.

But the words wouldn't come. He couldn't quite shake the doubts that were forming now. So much of what they were saying did make sense, as much as he hated it. He closed his eyes again.

'We understand why this all must come as a bit of a bombshell,' Dee said, immediately regretting the turn of phrase.

Sam ignored it, or at least didn't register he'd caught it.

Dee surged on. 'You'll need time to process it all. But time doesn't wait for the truth, Sam. It never has, and every second you put off the inevitable, someone else is getting hurt.'

Sam's eyes opened again. 'But I'm a complete nobody. Jason even said it himself. I'm boring. Ordinary. What the hell could I possibly do?'

Jason seized the moment. 'And it's precisely because you're ordinary that you'd make a perfect member of The Firm. You're above suspicion, beyond reproach. Trust me, they're not keen on hiring bad boys. You have a golden opportunity to do something. Take a few days off work to recover from your injuries. Seriously, you've been through a devastating incident and are lucky to be alive. You need to take some time to recover. But that'll also give you time to assess all we've been saying. Then next week, or the week after that, go back to your job. Look into some of the things we'll tell you about. See for yourself from the inside. I guarantee you'll be blown away. It's not pretty, Sam. We've only told you about the latest false flag attack. But there've been more. There'll always be more.'

Dee adored Sam's son, Benjamin. They'd visited him together in Edinburgh several times over the last couple of years, and they'd become close. She knew he was a bright kid with an amazing future ahead of him. Mentioning him again now could make or break the situation. Dee took a chance. She had to.

'And think of Benji. I know you don't want to sit back and watch on as Benji grows up in a world of corruption and government-sponsored atrocities. How could you?'

Unbidden, a tear formed in the corner of Sam's eye. It all sounded so far-fetched as to be beyond belief. But if it wasn't far-fetched — if they were right and were simply telling him the truth — then he couldn't ignore it. How could he? He had a son. He had a duty to protect his son and the mother of his only child. Sure, he'd been doing it from afar for the last seventeen years.

But now he saw that wasn't enough. Not nearly enough.

He had to do more.

26

Dee and Jason watched Sam as he appeared to be silently considering what they were saying. Dee might have been wrong, but she had a hunch Sam was ready to talk.

'Sam, please listen to me. I know how it must look, bearing in mind our situation. Me and you, I mean. But I promise you now, I wasn't using you. I love you. You know I do. But there are bigger things happening here. More important things. I know what a valuable member of The Firm you'd be. Jason obviously felt the same way.'

Sam glanced at Jason, who nodded and held Sam's gaze.

'Sam, we go back a long way. More than a quarter of a century, can you believe that? I know your character. I know who you are. I've known since I saw you shove away the wood-work teacher in middle school. Mr Easton. Remember him? Dirty old fucker used to go around grabbing things he shouldn't have been grabbing. Bastard used to say shit like "Come in the cupboard and I'll give you a screw." Most of the kids didn't really understand what was happening. But not you. You were the first person I ever remember standing up to him. You were braver than the rest of us. Braver than me. I always respected you after that. I know you, Sam. You're one of the good guys, and god knows we need more of you on our team.'

Sam didn't know Jason was capable of such compliments. He did remember Mr Easton, though. He was a dirty bastard. Sam had shoved him away. He'd done more than that, too. He'd learned where Easton lived, and one night Sam had launched a brick through his window with a note attached to it. The words were simple:

DO NOT TOUCH ANY KIDS AGAIN OR I WILL KILL YOU

As far as Sam knew, Mr Easton had never laid a finger on another child again. Sam had known he was incapable of carrying out his ridiculous threat to kill him. But he'd felt he had to do something. And that something had apparently worked.

Both Dee and Jason had sensed a shift in Sam's attitude over the last few minutes. He no longer seemed in denial about what they'd told him. He'd definitely calmed down and didn't look as if he was about to pass out or throw up. They hadn't wanted to make it personal by bringing Benji into it. But it seemed to have had the right impact.

'When I was first approached,' Dee said, 'I didn't appreciate the scale of the corruption within our government. And it's not just this current government, either. Nothing has ever changed. They're all as bad as each other. But I didn't know that then. To be honest, I agreed to join because it sounded fun and exciting. I was pretty bored working at the Home Office and needed something else. And it was exciting. When you start realising how much good can be done and how many people are affected, it's a real buzz to help. It's important work, Sam. The most important work any of us will ever do.'

'Let me ask you a question,' Jason continued. 'Have you ever wondered why Anderson was so happy to see Michael Sullivan come to the office? When you go back into the office, do a little digging into Anderson. You'll see for yourself. The two are old friends. They share some shady secrets.'

Sam found himself shaking his head again, though he soon stopped as a nasty headache was starting to kick in. He downed the rest of his pint anyway.

Jason had one more angle to try. He hoped it wouldn't antagonise Sam too much. 'And, well, isn't it about time you began fulfilling your potential?' Jason said. 'Think about it. Look at the little things, even. Stopping you from going to see your son. Cancelling annual leave. It might not sound like much, but they're all small ways of turning the screw. Piece by piece, they'll have complete control. If you join The Firm you'll be able to put these fuckers down. And with the amount of shit happening every day in this country, you'll be guaranteed a job for life. Not only that, it's a job worthy of your ability, and you'll be compensated in accordance with those skills.'

Sam looked at Jason, a hint of confusion in his eyes.

Jason cocked his head a little. 'It's a really well-paid job is what I'm saying.' Jason grinned. Sam didn't. At least not externally. Well-paid was good. Good for Benji and Leila.

'But way more important than the money,' Dee pressed, 'is the knowledge you'll be helping people. Helping them from out of the shadows of corrupt governments. Helping give people back their civil liberties. Helping put an end to government-backed atrocities. Putting the right people behind bars instead of the —'

'Patsies? I get it,' Sam cut in, and it was the first positive thing he'd said since he'd arrived at The Barley Mow.

His resolve was weakening by the minute.

27

'I get it. Just give me a minute, okay?'

Dee and Jason nodded, and watched as Sam stood and looked out of the window. 'I need some air. Back in a minute.'

Sam walked to the door and stepped out into the overcast afternoon. When he'd entered the pub an hour before, it was sunny and warm outside. Now the sky was grey and the warmth had been replaced by a sticky humidity unusual for June. It was as if the weather matched his mood. Hazy. Muddled. Things seemed to be closing in around him, almost as if the next decision or choice he made might define his very future, maybe even his existence. The first spot of rain landed on his cheek. Then another. He ducked under the doorway of the pub and was about to step inside. He thought better of it. Instead, Sam left.

Despite the constant throbbing pain in his ribs, Sam broke into a half-walk half-jog until he was three streets away. Finally, he stopped under a bus shelter and paused, half expecting to see Jason sprinting after him. But no one was there, and as the rain began pelting down in ever-increasing torrents, Sam decided he didn't care, and walked the rest of the way home to his flat. The office could do without him for the rest of the day. Despite what The Firm thought, Sam knew he wasn't that important.

Twenty-five minutes after leaving the pub, Sam trudged up the stairs to his flat and let himself in. He kicked off his squelching shoes and tossed them in the shower cubicle. Then he stripped down to nothing, gulped several painkillers too many and climbed into the shower, turning the water as hot as he could bear in an effort to rinse away the shame he felt, a shame that came from a number of places.

He thought of Dee and Jason. If they were right, it meant he had to question everything he thought he knew. And if they were right, his government really was corrupt. He was ashamed of that, and it was a betrayal that would cut far too deep if proven true.

He was ashamed of his initial unwillingness to listen. Sure, what he'd been told by first Travers and Jason, then by Dee, was far-fetched. But they were adamant, and if correct, they were only trying to help. He should have been more open-minded. Should have been less willing to bury his head in the sand.

All these thoughts swirled around his addled mind as the near-scalding shower water did little to lift his mood. He stepped out of the glass cubicle and wiped the steamy mirror clear to look at himself as one more element of his ever-growing shame — the most important element — came barrelling to the fore. It was the well-deserved shame he would feel about himself if he didn't do something about all this. He had to give Jason and Dee the benefit of the doubt. They knew so much. There was rarely smoke without fire. There must be something to it. If not, it still had to be worth looking into, even if only to prove to himself — one way or another — that they were wrong.

He'd known they wouldn't follow him from the pub or try to stop him leaving. And he knew that because they knew he'd be back at some point. They'd seen it in his eyes, and just as he was sure they'd known he'd make the right decision, he also knew they too were right. He had made it. He couldn't just sit around when apparently so many others, including Jason, Dee and their boss, Tom Travers, were standing up to be counted. It was time for action.

It was time for Sam Barker to stand up and be counted.

Sam went through to his bedroom and threw on some clothes, then grabbed his laptop and slumped down on his sofa. It was time to do some research, one of the few things he had to admit he was very good at. His stomach growled audibly, and Sam trudged back into the kitchen, suddenly hungry. He swung open the fridge door, then paused.

Sam closed his eyes and shook his head, then slowly closed the door again, knowing what he'd find on the door even before he saw it properly.

It was another note, written in the same handwriting as the previous one. It was Dee's. Now Sam had worked out it was her writing, he couldn't believe he hadn't recognised it last time. Then again, she was supposed to have been in Wales. Was it all a lie? Had she ever told him the truth — until now?

He chose not to read it just yet, and put it back on the fridge door. Snagging some supplies from inside, he threw together a sandwich and made a cuppa, then grabbed the note and went back to the lounge. Sam was in no hurry to read it. He thought he already knew what it said. When his curiosity finally got the better of him, the sandwich half-eaten, he snatched up the note.

When he read it, he tried not to smile, but did anyway. It read:

I knew you'd see the light.
Time doesn't wait for the truth, does it?
Call me ASAP.
Dee

28

Before ringing Dee, Sam called Leila to check in on her and Benji. With everything he'd learned and had been through in the last few days, he felt the need to speak to them both as soon as possible, needed to know they were okay. Benji wasn't home, but Leila confirmed he was still loving uni, and that he was excelling at his environmental science course. His grades were good, and his professors had high hopes for him.

'At least we did something right, eh Sam?' Leila would often say, and it was true. Benji was an exceptional young man, and they were both very proud parents. Sam had called Leila from the hospital and told her about the bombing, and talked her into not flying to London immediately.

'Just give Benji a hug from me please, okay?' Sam said before ending the call. Relieved that the two most important people in his life were okay, Sam called Dee.

'I guess we need to talk,' Sam said after Dee answered. She'd picked up before the second ring.

'Yes, I think we do,' Dee agreed. 'But not over this line,

okay? Let's meet. Remember that pub we went to after Christmas drinks three years ago... on that night?'

Sam did remember. He'd never forget it. 'Of course I remember. What time?'

'See you at nine?'

And so at eight thirty five that night — twenty five minutes early — Sam walked into The Knights Templar pub on Chancery Lane, not at all surprised to see Dee sitting there already, a half-empty glass of white wine and a pint of what he assumed was London Pride on the table in front of her. He tried to suppress his grin, but it was a futile effort, so he let it happen. When she saw him approach, Dee stood from the table and smiled too, perhaps as widely as Sam had ever seen.

'I can't tell you how pleased I am to see you, Sam,' she said, leaning in for a hug. 'For many reasons.' She smiled, but it wasn't the open, warm smile Sam was used to seeing from his girlfriend. 'Please, have a seat.' It was a little more formal than Sam liked or expected.

'London Pride?' Sam asked. 'Never mind, don't answer that. Of course it's London Pride. What else could it be?' he asked quietly as he sat down. 'Some kind of code word?'

'Something like that. Appropriate, don't you think?'

'Cheesy is what I think. So...'

'So...'

This was going to be awkward.

'Okay, you have my attention,' Sam said. 'But I have to tell you, I'm going to need more than just a few scary stories to be totally convinced. I think that's fair, don't you?'

'Of course. But believe me when I say we've only scratched the surface with what we've told you up to this point. You'll need to be more open-minded than you've ever been, because it's not pretty. Not pretty at all.'

Sam sipped at his pint. This was the first time he'd been alone with Dee in a couple of weeks. They'd been seeing less of each other over the last couple of months, and Sam thought he finally realised why.

'I have to ask. Have you been avoiding me lately because of all this? I mean, because of The Firm?'

Dee gazed at Sam, who saw a definite hint of sadness and regret in her eyes. 'It's complicated. But yes, I'll be honest and say that's part of it. Can we talk about that later?'

Sam didn't answer. He inhaled deeply, and let out a slow breath. If he was going to lose the only woman he'd loved in the last decade and a half, she'd better have a damn good reason. He nodded, trying not to show his disappointment, but certain he'd failed.

'Before we get too far,' Dee said, 'there are some things you'll need to know.' She leaned in closer, though there was nobody else within earshot. The weather had worsened and it was miserable outside. Besides, apparently there was a new season of *Game of Thrones* on the box. Sam had never seen it himself — one of the few not to, he'd been told. But whatever floated other people's boats was fine with him.

'Let's just assume for a moment that you agree to join The Firm. You'd not technically be working for us, though you would be paid well for your service. It's important for now to stay on at your job. You're in an incredibly strategic situation for us right now,' Dee said. 'I know that sounds as if you're being used, but it's not like that at all. There are other people in similar jobs, and we've considered recruiting them. But they aren't you. Tom Travers wants you for a reason.'

Sam sipped his pint again. He was all ears.

'The access you have to all those databases is an unprecedented opportunity for us to gather evidence against the people we know are a threat to this country from the inside. I'm talking about politicians, obviously, but it's not only politicians. It's industry leaders. Local officials. Top-ranking military brass, as well as those at the head of law enforcement. News and media outlets. Mayors. Members of the Boards of Education. Housing Associations. Even school, college and university examining bodies aren't beyond fixing data for their own benefit. Sam, there are hardly any sectors in this country, both government and private, that aren't in some way corrupted by individuals or groups of people who don't care anything about the welfare of the people they represent, but instead make their decisions and rules based on their own insatiable greed for wealth or power — usually both.'

Sam listened carefully, trying to absorb all Dee was saying. Despite his reticence to accept it all, Sam wasn't naive. He loved his country, and that love might have had the ability to blind him to some things. Perhaps it was more a case of him hiding from the truth. That certainly wasn't uncommon. And it didn't make Sam a bad person. But was it right? Would things ever improve if people turned a blind eye to what happened in the world? Well, those questions were easy to answer. No, it wasn't right. And no, things would never improve.

It was Sam's turn to speak. 'Let's assume for a moment that I join The Firm.'

Dee smiled at Sam's use of her phrase. 'I'll humour you only because you humoured me.'

'Exactly. So, if I joined The Firm, would you give me assignments? I mean, you keep mentioning my position at the Home

Office as if it's key to all this. Is it? And I understand I'll be reporting directly to Travers, and that we all work for him. Right?'

'Wrong. I report to Travers, as does Jason.' Dee took a sip of her drink. 'You, however, will report to me.'

THE GUARDIAN

16TH JUNE

ANTI-MUSLIM HATE CRIMES AT ALL TIME HIGH, SAYS NEW SURVEY

Recent figures released in the wake of the Westminster bombings show hate crimes directed at members of the Muslim community are at an all-time high, according to a report published by Stop Hate UK.

The figures show that seven London mosques have been vandalised in recent days, in apparent revenge attacks for the terrorist atrocities which saw forty-six people lose their lives.

The report details how one imam was physically assaulted in the street outside his mosque, with a man pinning him to a wall, spitting in his face and calling him a 'fucking paki'.

At one Brixton school, parents received a letter warning them to ensure their children were escorted to and from school until further notice, after reports that two Asian pupils at the school had been verbally and physically assaulted on their way home. Both are Hindu.

The report makes mention of other incidents in which people of other Asian minority groups have been targeted in the apparent — but false — belief they were Muslims.

Regardless, with three million Muslim citizens currently living in Britain, and only seven Muslim-related terrorist incidents having occurred in the entire history of the country, it is at best questionable as to how severe the threat truly is.

There can be no doubt that Muslim extremism exists, as it does in all other religions. But the truth remains that there have been more incidents of white nationalist terrorism in Britain in recent years than any other form of reported extremism.

With recent comments by the likes of Michael Sullivan stoking racial tensions further, it seems to be a foregone conclusion that attacks from — and on — both sides are likely to continue and escalate.

29

Sam awoke early, glad to have dodged a hangover. He didn't drink much anymore, but the rare occasions he did usually provided him with a thick head and a morning's worth of regret the following day — especially if it was a working day.

Well, today was such a day, but it was unlike any day at work he'd ever known. He'd taken the bus to the office due to the persistent drizzle that shrouded London like a widow's veil and, as per usual, he'd arrived early. After a couple of half-hearted hellos from people who didn't usually notice him but who probably felt sorry for him after the bombing, he'd grabbed a coffee from the staff café and plonked himself down at his desk.

It immediately felt different to normal. It looked the same. The desk and seat were the same desk and seat. His PC and monitor were the same. In essence, everything was just as it was before the bombing. But it felt far from that. Very far from that indeed.

Everyone Sam could see across the vast office space was

now a potential liar, and he hated himself for thinking it. From good old Roger Goulder in IT Support, who ran the weekly National Lottery syndicate to stuffy old Janet Barlow in Accounts. Was Roger skimming off the weekly lottery collections? Was Jan cooking the books?

How about Peter Graham in Analytics? PG was always first in line to make collections for people's birthdays and retirement gifts. Was he on the take? And what about Scott Adams in Legal? Scottie was the office joker, and he also ran the weekly pools collection. Was he lining his pockets? Did anyone ever actually check whether the pools had come in or not?

And what about Lucy, the one genuine friend Sam believed he had from work, other than Dee? At thirty, Lucy was one of the youngest workers in the office, and easily the most popular. She was definitely the prettiest. Was she up to no good? Sam now wondered if her jovial, flirty nature was all just a cover for less harmonious, less scrupulous activities.

Sam no longer knew, and he no longer trusted his judgment. But one thing he did know was that unless he was careful, all this would drive him insane.

He'd left Dee at the pub last night with a promise he would give her his answer before the end of the week. She'd reminded him at least twice that time didn't wait for the truth. It was almost cliché. She was probably right. But Sam was insistent; if he was going to make the biggest decision of his life, he wanted — and needed — time to get it right.

He'd escaped a hangover, but by late morning his head ached. He threw down a few more painkillers and walked to the bathroom to splash water on his face. Standing in front of the mirror, Sam stared at his reflection for a few seconds. He looked older than he remembered. Tired. Gaunt. *Damn, I need a holiday*, he thought, but it lacked conviction. If he was going to do this, he doubted he'd get a break any time soon.

He continued staring at the figure in the mirror, unsure who was staring back. It certainly wasn't himself. Not the quiet, likeable but aloof Sam Barker. Not Mr Reliable. Not the guy in the office who, when Scottie reminded him he hadn't paid his pools money — even though Sam was certain he had — had paid again anyway, just so it wouldn't cause a fuss.

And the longer he stared at that stranger in the mirror, the more Sam realised he didn't like him. *When did I get to be so weak? When did I become the guy who let the world pass him by? Why am I such a fucking nobody?*

From some unknown well of emotion, Sam started to weep. It was just a couple of tears at first, which he wiped away with his sleeve. But then more came, and he could do nothing to stop them. He hustled into one of the toilet cubicles and locked the door. He sat down and leant forward, resting his forehead in both palms. And there he let the tears flow.

Sam hadn't cried like that for years. He couldn't even remember the last time he'd shed any tears at all. He hadn't even cried when Yasmin died before his eyes on the Underground, or when he thought of his distraught and heartbroken friend, Malik, whose life would never, ever be the same again.

So why was he so upset now? But Sam knew the answer. He knew it with such force and certainty that it was as if he had always known it. It was because he was ashamed. So very, very ashamed. He'd become the guy he despised without even realising it. He had been burying his head in the sand to avoid the truth. He'd hidden behind it for so long that he had lost sight of what was true, what was so obvious now that he could scarcely refrain from punching himself around the head.

He really didn't know anything any more. If his friends had been lying to him for years, who else had he mistakenly trusted? What other institutions he'd always taken for granted weren't what they seemed? What other unquestionable facts and truths were not what he thought they were? The more he pondered this, the more disheartened he became.

But the one thing that cut the deepest wasn't the fact Jason and Dee had been lying to him. Assuming they were telling him the truth, they were acting in his — and the country's — best interests. He should probably be grateful.

No. Sam was hurt most by the fact that The Firm even needed to exist. It meant his government, the institution he'd put his faith and trust in since he was first able to vote as an eighteen-year-old student, had lied to him. All those years he'd played by their rules. All those times he'd voted. All those times he'd told himself he might not necessarily agree with the politicians' decisions, but that they had the best interests of the country at heart.

It hurt Sam. Hurt him a lot. It was the ultimate betrayal for someone who had trusted his government and believed in them unconditionally and without prejudice. Sam wasn't fiercely political. But he watched the international news most days and watched on as, around the world, governments collapsed and countries' economies failed because of corruption or military coups.

Britain had always been safe, and Sam had never felt that safety more than when his own father was in the British Army. Tony Barker had been fighting for the liberation of the Falklands when Sam was born, and later saw active service in the

Gulf. Whereas most children might have worried about their fathers entering a war zone, Sam had instead felt that the presence of his father would make those areas safe. This proud, fiercely patriotic man had been his hero.

Sam had always believed citizens of other countries were envious of Britain. After all, they still had the world's best healthcare system and some of the most prestigious education establishments anywhere on the planet.

But was he wrong? Had he been misled all this time? Were the failings his own? Had he been so blinded by loyalty that he'd sat by and done nothing, all the while being lied to?

Sam's head ached. He left the bathroom and stalked back to his desk. He didn't speak to anyone, or rather, no one spoke to him — nothing unusual there.

He grabbed his things and shoved them in his bag, before striding out of the office, riding the lift down to the lobby in silence and stepping out onto a rainy, windswept street. By the time he got home he was soaked through and shivering from the unseasonable cold. He showered and changed, and sat at his tiny kitchen table, staring at his mobile phone. He stared at it for a full ten minutes, hardly taking his eyes off it as his mind swirled and his heart raced.

Sam had made his decision. He had thought it was going to be the hardest decision of his life, harder even than letting go of Benji and Leila. Harder even than leaving her to bring up their baby son alone all those years ago. He'd always thought nothing could possibly be harder than that, yet he'd believed this would be.

But in the end it was easy. The truth had come at him with such clarity that it had turned out to be the easiest choice he'd ever made. He had made his decision. And it was time to tell those that needed to know.

Grabbing his mobile phone, he called the new number Dee had given him. He had told her he needed until the end of the week. But somehow Sam knew Dee would be expecting his call today.

30

Thankfully the following day was Saturday, meaning Sam wasn't expected at the office. The weekend would give him a little breathing space, because he knew that when he arrived back at his desk on Monday his objectives would be vastly different. He would still fulfil all the expected duties of his genuine employer, the Home Office, and his boss, Frank Anderson. But Sam knew that even operating at just fifty-percent commitment he would achieve those goals, and with plenty of room to spare. He'd been coasting through his duller-than-dishwater job for months anyway, and could more or less carry out his tasks with his eyes closed. Sam knew he would have plenty of time each day to carry out his new, more important objectives: those given to him by Dee and Jason.

The pair visited Sam at his flat in Waterloo on Saturday afternoon, joined by Tom Travers. It was an informal meeting — how could an organisation that didn't officially exist have anything but informal meetings, Sam mused when Dee had called to arrange it. Yet Sam sensed by the mirthless manner in which the three of them arrived that this was serious business.

'May I start by saying,' Travers said, 'that we're happy to have you on board. As you know, we take our recruitment very seriously. Based on what I've been told by Jason and Dee, and what I've researched about you myself, we have high hopes for you.'

Sam sat quietly and listened to Travers. The boss of the British branch of The Firm exuded confidence and control, and seemed to have earned the complete respect of both Jason and Dee. Despite himself, Sam was impressed by Tom Travers.

Which was good, because he'd just agreed to work for the man.

'I want to echo Tom's words.' Jason said, fixing his eyes on Sam. 'I'm very glad you're with us. Dee and I have been working on this for some time, and I know it will be worth it.' Just the hint of a smile at his old friend. 'I know you've agreed to join us, and help us in our mission to expose and bring down the corrupt members of our government and other powerful organisations. The fact you've joined us means you must've accepted what we've told you as fact, however difficult that was. But that's just the first step. Now you're going to have to back that step up with many more decisions, each tougher than the last. For example, for every guilty person we expose, it's likely innocent people are going to suffer. Unsuspecting spouses. Their children. Innocent organisations that relied upon that person might crumble without them. We do all we can to protect those unfortunate people and institutions when we expose or remove the corruption, but sometimes it's impossible. That's something you're going to have to understand and deal with when the time comes.'

Sam nodded. 'I understand.'

'I know you do. You wouldn't be here if you didn't.'

'There are other factors too.' Dee smiled, but it faded quickly. 'Sometimes it's more than that. Sometimes we remove one cog of the corrupt machine, and that cog gets replaced by something worse. Sometimes we have to accept that retribution is a real possibility. People get hurt, Sam. Occasionally sacrifices need to be made. It's the nature of it. I wish it were as simple as saying something like "sacrifice the few for the good of the many," but it isn't that simple. It never is. Do you understand what I'm trying to say?'

Sam stared at Dee. Until just a few weeks ago Sam and Dee were in what Sam considered a fairly serious relationship, though it had eased up a little in recent months, the reasons for which were now becoming clear. And yet here she was in his flat, sitting on the same sofa on which they'd shared numerous bottles of wine, upon which they'd watched dozens of movies and where they'd occasionally got naked. The context in which Dee sat there now could not have been more different.

'I think I understand,' Sam answered. 'For example, you never coming here for a social visit again.' He smirked, but no one smiled. 'Listen, I know. I get that now. By sacrifices, you mean people actually get hurt, maybe even die. Is that it?'

'Yes. Sometimes people die. Thankfully we haven't had to take it that far too often here in the UK, though it's happened. In Eastern Europe, and especially in some war-torn African nations... Well, let's just say that The Firm sometimes has to go to somewhat more extreme measures to do the right thing.'

Sam nodded again. He did understand. 'Look, I know what I'm signing up for. I do. And I'm ready for it.' Sam took a deep breath before asking, 'What is it you want me to do?'

31

'Oh, is that all? Why didn't you say so? Candy from a baby.' Sam stood up and paced around his modest living room, clenching and unclenching his fists while the others watched on. It would have been amusing if it wasn't so serious. 'Piece of cake. Just to be clear, you want me to dig the dirt on Sullivan to stop him coming to power and potentially bring down the entire British government? No problem. Why don't I just get straight to it? Probably take a few hours, but we'll get there. Save the world while I'm at it, should I?'

Sam slumped back into the armchair, his mind foggy and his pulse racing. Were they serious? But as he looked into Dee's eyes, then glanced first at Jason and then Travers, they all looked back at him, unsmiling, unflinching and unperturbed by his outburst. He figured they must have seen similar reactions before. And yes, they were all deadly serious.

'Are you even going to tell me what I'm supposed to be looking for?' he asked.

'I'm afraid we can't do that,' Jason replied.

'Are you serious? Surely you've got to give me something to

go on. How am I meant to know what you want from me otherwise?'

'We can't risk tainting your views at this stage,' Dee said. 'Sometimes you can know too much. You can't go in with pre-knowledge which might affect the way you look for information. It's best that anything you find is pure and arrived at in a natural way.'

Sam let out a laugh. 'You can't risk tainting my views? You've literally just turned all of my views completely upside down. You've thrown these conspiracy theories at me without even telling me what they are, told me everything I know is a lie and now you expect me to prove it without any extra informa-tion or guidance whatsoever?' He sat up and placed his hands on his thighs. After a couple of deep breaths, he calmed down. 'Okay, listen, I'm sorry. It's just, well, you know... a bit heavy for a first assignment, isn't it?'

'Listen, Sam. I know it's a lot to take in. Of course it is. And we know it's all happening so quickly. We've done this many times before and we know there'll be an adjustment period. You'll have to reconsider many things you thought you knew, both about individual people and larger institutions, many of them household names. You'll also need to foster rela-tionships with certain colleagues we know you have. But we can talk about that later. It's one of the hardest parts of the job.'

'You mean using people? Because I feel pretty used right now.'

'It could be phrased that way, yes. But think of the bigger picture. You'll need to leave all ego and selfishness aside for this to work. We've all had to do it. I've had to do it.' Dee looked hard at Sam as she said that, as if she needed him to understand she hadn't used him and that she had genuinely cared about him. Though it didn't really matter any more.

Sam just nodded. He got it. Didn't mean he had to like it. And he didn't.

'At the same time, you're going to have to live as you lived before. Same routines. Same out-of-work activities. Same —'

Sam scoffed at that one. 'You know very well I don't have out-of-work activities,' he said, and stared at Dee so hard she had to look away.

'You know what she means,' Jason said. 'Look, we've all had to make sacrifices, mate. Every member of The Firm has made them. But we do it because we know how important it is. The fact you don't have much of a social life is a big advantage. The fewer people you're close to, the fewer people there are to keep secrets from. The fewer people to hurt.' Jason looked away himself. Because of his role in The Firm, someone very dear to him had made the ultimate sacrifice. He'd never forgiven himself, but it was the nature of the beast and he coped the best way he could — by continuing the pursuit for justice.

It had happened almost five years earlier. Jason's wife, Penny, was a special-needs teacher at a school in west London. Through his work with The Firm, Jason had uncovered a terror plot involving Azim Al Huq, a known terrorist and one of the main people associated with the cell in Balham involving Abdul Wahid Mohammed, the man framed as the perpetrator of the recent Underground bombing. Al Huq had avoided capture, but someone had learned Jason's identity. In what could only be described as a callous revenge attack, Penny was abducted on her way home from the school. Her body was found cut up in a skip at the school the following morning. It had been reported as a senseless murder, but the simple postcard Jason received in the post a few days later told him otherwise. The two word message was clear: *From Allah.*

Jason had never really got over the loss of this wife, but in the years since he'd devoted his entire life to ridding his country of corruption and seeking retribution for her death.

Sam had met Penny a few times and was devastated when he heard she'd been murdered. But he had never heard anything about who was responsible. Until two days ago he had never even heard of The Firm. As he looked at Jason's pained expression now, he was beginning to think there was more to her death than he'd previously known.

His thoughts immediately turned to Benji and Leila. By getting involved in all this, would he be putting the two people he cared about most in the world at risk? It seemed that way. But what if he didn't try and help? Well, they were already at risk in this crazy world.

What kind of world was this? he silently mused. Was he a spy? The phrase might have struck Sam as funny if it wasn't so serious. It was the first time he'd thought of it that way. But that's what he was being asked to do, wasn't it? Spy on his colleagues? Spy on the future Prime Minister?

Several names came to mind. Bond. Bourne. Barker? It almost seemed like a joke. He was no James Bond. For a start, Bond was handsome and always got the girls. If anything, Sam knew he was the very antithesis of James Bond. And Bourne? Well, if he was unlike Bond he was the complete opposite of Jason Bourne. Hard bastard. Always knew what to do. Could probably make a bomb out of an egg box. The only thing Sam could make was a decent Sunday roast, though he never even made those anymore after some stern words from Benji.

How was it that he'd been recruited for a top-secret organisation, who allegedly had the power to bring down governments and save the country? If he'd doubted his worth for such things before, he knew now without any shadow of a doubt that he was totally and utterly out of his depth.

Tom Travers had watched on quietly as Dee and Jason had been discussing business with their newest recruit. He saw the doubt in the man's eyes. It was true Travers needed to be convinced of anyone's credentials and suitability when it came to working with The Firm. But Dee and Jason, two of Travers's closest and most trusted assets, had both been adamant about him.

At first glance, Sam Barker didn't seem much. Physically average, but above average intellect. Decent education. Squeaky-clean character, which was usually a good thing. But Tom Travers liked to know he could rely on his assets when the shit hit the fan. He knew, for example, that both Dee and Jason could handle almost any situation, including physical, if it came to it. But he saw no evidence Barker was made of the same stuff. Still, they could work on that side of things later. He trusted Dee and Jason. Their judgments had never let either themselves, nor The Firm, down before, and both were integral cogs in everything they did out of their London-based operation.

So Travers had trusted them again, this time with Sam Barker. He couldn't deny Barker's strategic position at the Home Office was a fortuitous prospect. Of course, they already had access to most of what Sam could find through his job. But they needed someone with that extra reach, that added slice of magic they'd yet to find in any of their recruits. Tom Travers was hopeful Sam was the man to take the British leg of The Firm to the next level. And it had to start now.

'Sam, it's natural to have doubts,' Travers said. 'We all do, at least about ourselves. But Dee and Jason have absolutely no doubts about you. You're one of us now. You have a duty to make the most of this rare opportunity to make our country a better place. Make the world a better place. Does it sound dramatic? Probably. Is it an understatement? Absolutely not.

'Sam, listen to this next part carefully. If Michael Sullivan becomes Prime Minister after the general election, and is allowed to shape the government to his dangerously flawed will, it will be bad for all of us. Bad for me. Bad for you. Bad for all our families, and for those millions of families around the country who don't know any better. Worst of all, it will be bad for our nation's children. Think of Benjamin. Let's make a difference for your son. Let's work together and give him a future in which he can thrive.'

Sam looked at Tom Travers. There was something about the man Sam couldn't put his finger on. He was a natural leader, sure. But not in the strong, commanding sense. Travers exuded an aura of confidence, a sense of loyalty to a cause Sam hadn't felt for anything in a long time.

Sam stood up. Dee, Jason and Tom Travers stood up too.

'I don't know if I have to make any kind of formal declaration,' Sam said, 'but I'll say this. I understand everything you've said to me this morning and over the last few days. I know there'll be sacrifices I need to make. I appreciate that my life will never be the same again from this day forward. I understand that any relationships I've had or will have in the future will become secondary to the important work I have to do for the greater good of the country. And I know that some of my actions may have serious consequences for many people, some of them undeserving of it.' He paused and took a few deep breaths. If it wasn't such a serious movement he was getting involved with, his words might have seemed silly. But they didn't, not to him, and not to the others standing there listening to them.

He held out his hand, first to Dee. She shook it, and the hint of a smile crinkled her eyes. Next Jason shook his hand, and it was firm and true. Finally, Sam offered his hand to Tom Travers, who stepped forward and clasped it formally in his own.

'For the greater good,' Sam said.

Silently, however, he wondered what he was getting himself into.

32

'You'll be needing these.'

Travers and Jason had left the flat, and only Sam and Dee remained. With those handshakes, Sam was now an unofficial, official member of The Firm. It was time for Dee to fill Sam in on some of the finer details.

She opened a folder and laid it down on the glass coffee table in front of them. She handed Sam a bank card. 'This is yours. It's a credit card with unlimited funds available to use however you need them.'

Sam glanced at Dee, his eyes wide. 'Like what?'

'Use it however you like. You might find you need to bribe reporters, or pay a photographer for some special photos, that kind of thing. If you need cash, draw it out on this card.'

Sam nodded. He'd been doing a lot of nodding lately, and knew it was because he simply hadn't known what to say most of the time. This was all so crazy. But he couldn't deny it — some of it sounded fun.

Dee handed him a small piece of plastic.

'What's that?' he asked, looking at it but not taking it.

'It's a SIM card, Sam. For your mobile phone. Pre-programmed with a few numbers you might need. The names are anonymised but should be fairly self-explanatory. They're named according to what you might need. Take DATA, for example. That guy will get you anyone's home address, who they bank with — he'll probably be able to find out their favourite crisp flavour.'

'Is it secure?'

'As secure as it'll ever be. It's registered to a company — one of many we operate to fly under the radar. But that's all you need to know for now. You'll need to use it in your own phone whenever you need to contact someone. It'd be too risky giving you a dedicated mobile, particularly bearing in mind the security measures at work. There's no way you'd get away with it.'

'Right. And what am I meant to be doing with this? Whose addresses and crisp flavours am I meant to be finding out exactly? Are you going to give me any names?'

'No. You'll work it out soon enough. It's better you don't have have any preconceived ideas before you begin looking. That's never a good idea. It'll make you act differently around people.'

Sam had been expecting that, and he hadn't stopped thinking about his co-workers since it had first crossed his mind. For now, he ignored it.

'You'll also need this.' Dee handed Sam a tiny USB drive. 'If the time comes to quickly download data or files from either your own computer or a colleague's, this drive will send it immediately to our database at the location in Crystal Palace. You know, where you —'

'I know. Spent a lovely and cosy few hours. I remember.'

He wasn't smiling, but Dee thought she noticed at least a

tiny trace of humour in Sam's eyes. That was good. She adored
Sam for his honesty and his all-round goodness, and they had
laughed a lot over the last three years. She'd miss it. Miss him.
She knew they were over now. Now Sam was in The Firm, it
was both impractical and unprofessional to be in a relationship
with him, however sad it was. It was just one more sacrifice she
knew they'd have to make. She focused on the task at hand.

'When you're back in the office Monday morning, what are
you going to do?'

'Aside from drinking seven double espressos and wondering
which of my so-called colleagues is a corrupt super-villain?'

'Aside from that.' Dee's eyes crinkled in a grin. She was
relieved Sam was finally on board. He could be the missing link
to take things forward — the breakthrough Dee and Jason
believed they needed — and she was confident that with his skill
set, and with the other operatives they already had in place, they
would have many future successes. They would start with Sullivan. There were dozens of other missions to get underway.
Perhaps hundreds. But for now, as far as the near-future of
Britain was concerned, Michael Sullivan was public enemy
number one.

'I usually have about four or five hours of my own work to
get through in any given day. It's actually double that, but you
know—'

'We know. You've very good. Hence...' Dee grinned.

'I can stagger that work throughout the day. I'll do some
digging around into Sullivan's past. I'm not especially comfortable with that, but I know it needs to be done. I think you're
right, by the way. I've always had a hunch as to what sort of
character Sullivan is. What sort of man can wear those shiny
suits and not be a bastard? I'll find what you want.'

'What we need,' she corrected. 'Trust me when I say he's worse than you think. A lot worse. You'll see that for yourself soon enough. Once you've uncovered enough hard evidence against him, we'll work out how to proceed from there. But just get that evidence, Sam, okay? The Firm needs you. Together we'll take the bastard down.'

Sam looked at Dee. Two years ago, if someone would've told him she was an asset working for a covert operation, like something out of a Lee Child book, he'd have laughed them all the way to the madhouse. But now? Now Sam saw in her things he'd never seen before. She was always a tough cookie. But now he sensed a deeper side, perhaps even a darker side. She was unafraid of anything. She was steely. Determined. Prepared to put her career on the line, obviously. Prepared to put her life on the line? Prepared to die for her country? Yes. Sam believed she was.

Did that mean he would have to be prepared to do the same? Well, he guessed it did.

Could he, though? Could the nobody that was Sam Barker really give up his life for the benefit of the country? Right then, sitting on his uncomfortable armchair in his modest flat in a dismal, rainy Waterloo, he honestly didn't know.

33

The rest of the weekend passed by in a blur. Sam had another chat with Leila, and a wonderfully long and uplifting conversation with Benji, which resulted in Sam promising his son he'd do his best to become vegan, although Sam suspected it was a promise he'd fail to keep. He wasn't an especially emotional man, neither was he known for his outpourings of love. But after all that had happened, and after his world had been turned upside down, first by the Westminster bombing and second by all the stuff with The Firm, he felt now more than ever he had to remind his son how much he loved him.

He spent Sunday doing a little housekeeping, both in his flat and online. Sam was usually a stickler for cleanliness, probably bordering on OCD, but things had understandably gotten away from him a little. He was happy to tidy up. Organising his bank accounts, however, was something he hated, but he did that too. He also looked up train tickets for Edinburgh for the global warming summit he'd promised Benji he'd go to. Whatever happened with Sam and The Firm between now and then, he would not let his son down.

He took a couple of long walks along the Thames, and went to pay his respects to his friend Malik. He wanted — needed — to tell Malik that Yasmin didn't seem to be in too much pain when she passed. But he didn't say that. He didn't want Malik to feel guilty that he wasn't there himself. Instead, Sam simply told his friend how sorry he was, and that he somehow knew whoever was responsible would pay. 'If there's anything you need...' he'd said before he left, but he knew there was nothing he could say that could possibly help Malik in any way.

So, before Sam knew it, he was at his desk at the Home Office on Monday morning, the first one there, and was already finishing his third cappuccino before the first awkward moment of the day sashayed up to his desk. Lucy.

Lucy's nature was naturally playful. Sam had given himself multiple pep talks since Dee had left his flat late on Saturday afternoon. He'd worried that he wouldn't be able to act normally once he arrived at the office again. After all, whether he liked it or not, everyone was now under suspicion. But he couldn't give off any hint that he was about to be investigating some of them, even though, other than his immediate boss, Frank Anderson, he had no idea yet as to who would be on The Firm's list.

His pep talks were designed to install certain rules in himself. He could never ask any of the office staff any questions he wouldn't normally ask them. To be fair, that ruled out almost everything. He also couldn't show any more interest than normal about how their weekends were, nor should he ask about their families. Quite honestly, he wasn't really interested anyway, since he counted very few of them as friends. To ask now would be so far against the grain that it would surely throw suspicion back on Sam.

He realised he was probably overthinking it, which he'd always had a nasty habit of doing with everything. Nevertheless, this wasn't any kind of situation he'd ever experienced before, and it wasn't as if he'd had months of intensive training before starting his first 'assignment'. They'd told him that he'd have to 'act normal'. Dee had given him a practical demonstration of how to set up the listening devices and how to connect to The Firm's databases. Indeed, it was as simple as she'd said it would be. But that was about it. Clearly they had more faith in him than he did of himself.

And so as Lucy waltzed over to him, he focused on acting normally as he wondered if his friend of the last year or two was on Dee's watch list.

'Morning Lucy. Did you have a... The weekend. Was it good?' He stumbled a little. *Bad start, Sam*, he thought.

Lucy's smile slipped away. 'You okay, Sam? You look a little pale. Hangover? Can I get you something?'

Sam felt ridiculous. Of course Lucy wasn't on the list. She was the nicest person in the office and would do anything for anyone. She always started the week as she meant to go on; happy, lively and a bundle of energy. It's how she got herself through the week. Sam knew he could have learned a thing or two from Lucy when she first started at the Home Office several years ago. He chided himself, took a deep breath and recovered.

'I'm fine. Thanks. I... Yes, I had a late night. Caught up with an old friend at the weekend.' At least that part was true. 'I'm fine, really. How are you?'

Lucy beamed. 'Actually, I'm very good, thanks for asking. I'll tell you about it sometime. Coffee?' It wasn't Lucy's duty to make coffee for the other staff, but she was outstanding at her job, and she knew everyone's coffee order off by heart. Her enthusiasm got many of the overworked, underpaid staff through their own miserable weeks.

Sam didn't need another coffee. He'd already had three. 'Sure,' he said anyway. 'Usual, please. Extra sugar. Thanks.'

Lucy swirled away and practically floated across the office, taking several more coffee orders before disappearing into the staff café.

Once she was out of sight, Sam shook his head then rubbed his chin. *First test failed*, he mused, and winced internally. This was going to be harder than he thought.

The first day came and went in a flurry of activity. It was four o'clock before he knew it, and when he'd finally finished his actual chores he figured there wasn't any time to start conducting any underhanded digging. That was fine. Sam decided he'd start tomorrow.

But being in the office that day had given him pause for thought. There were close to forty people in that one vast office space. Sam knew half of them by their first names. Half of those he knew a little about, such as how many kids they had and what car they drove. He even knew a couple of them supported Chelsea, which immediately ruled them off any non-existent Christmas card list. Nobody liked Chelsea. Not even Chelsea fans.

A handful of them he actually liked. Dee, obviously. Lucy, the effervescent bundle of energy, who aside from Dee was his only proper friend at work. A guy named Gordon who, as a Spurs fan was good for banter, especially if Arsenal won at the weekend. That left around twenty people Sam knew not the first thing about. Sam knew he'd soon be delving into the private lives of several members of his office. He hoped he was wrong, but he had an overwhelming sense — The Firm had confirmed it as fact — someone who worked within fifty feet of him on a daily basis was up to no good.

34

Technology had always fascinated Sam. His father had always been an early adopter of new technologies, being one of the first people in their area to own a home computer.

He recalled those early days, watching the flickering glass monitor as it displayed the BASIC code he typed into the heavy cream-coloured keyboard.

The coding language's name now seemed rather prescient, but at the time it was revolutionary. Typing in a series of fairly simple commands resulted in the machine drawing shapes, automating tasks and even producing simple games.

It was beautiful. Romantic. Everyone knew it was a sign of things to come, but there was no way they could have predicted the scale and speed of growth: that the average person would now possess — in their own pocket — computing power many times greater than the machines that put man on the moon.

The very fundamentals of modern day computing — social media, smartphones, the cloud — were barely conceivable in the days when Sam would sit in his parents' spare bedroom, slavishly writing code and perfecting his craft.

He recalled an old saying that one should never mix business with pleasure, and it had struck him on more than one occasion that he had begun to enjoy his job less and less over the years. But he was now starting to realise that wasn't strictly true.

It hadn't been the job itself, or the fact he was getting paid to do what he loved — it was that he was now restricted, following tasks set by higher powers, working within a set framework. And it was enacting his own renegade tasks for The Firm which made him realise it.

It hadn't taken long for the realisation to set in. From the moment he'd first logged onto the Home Office network after agreeing to help The Firm, he felt alive. Alive for the first time in years. He wasn't just there as an employee, doing the government's bidding; he was working under his own volition, trying to unlock a route for The Firm to seek the truth — seek justice.

It was easier said than done. Anything digital could never be entirely secure, but there were ways and means. Sam knew that any defence was only as good as its weakest link. The Home Office's technology infrastructure funding had been channelled largely into trying to avert and subvert cyber terrorism and outside attacks. The focus had been on wider networks and making sure everything was kept in-house.

That meant the weakness would be within.

He recalled The Firm having alluded to cover-ups in the past, and to records having been erased. He also knew that data was rarely erased in its entirety.

The nature of the storage drives used at the Home Office — and in most hard drives — meant that there was technically never any empty space. Data could be overwritten, but never erased. Whenever a file or series of data was deleted, it was simply made inaccessible and appeared to be 'free', whereas in reality it remained on the hard drive, marked available, ready and waiting for new data to overwrite it. That meant it was entirely conceivable that any deleted data or records could still be in at least partial existence.

It was true that entire hard drives and storage devices could be effectively wiped by overwriting the drive dozens or hundreds of times over, making the original data irretrievable, but that would have meant someone ruining an entire drive's worth of data — something Sam found unlikely.

The coding for his homemade program had only taken him a few hours to put together. It was designed to index and search all fragments of data on a given hard drive or storage device — including deleted fragments which were available for over-writing.

It would then determine what type of file it had originally formed a part of, before rendering any salvageable text or data in a way which could be read or viewed.

It was also able, in a rudimentary way, to piece together frag-ments of data which had previously been linked or part of the same data set. This had been the trickiest aspect to code, and Sam knew it wouldn't be perfect. However, it was an algorithm he could refine and perfect at a later date if needed.

Towards the end of the day, once the program was ready, he granted it access to the Home Office's central data storage and entered his first search term: *Sullivan*.

He knew from the sheer enormity of the storage system and the relatively slow processing speed of his office computer that the search would take many hours, if not longer.

Swallowing and taking a deep breath, he hit the Enter key, locked his computer and went home.

· · ·

The next morning, Sam woke with a start. His first thought on waking was remembering what he'd done the previous day. He was sure he'd covered his tracks, but how certain could he really be?

Creating an in-house program to search for missing data fragments could easily be explained. There were a plethora of potential security uses for that. Testing it on his own machine, on the Home Office's own storage servers, was the natural first step. And the search term? Well, what was wrong with the likely future Prime Minister's name being front and centre of a Home Office employee's mind?

Those rationalisations still didn't go far towards putting Sam's mind at ease, though, and he made his way into the office without even stopping for breakfast. He wanted to get in, see if his program had worked and then delete the bloody thing. It had been a stupid idea. There was too much at risk. What the hell was he doing trying to pry on confidential Home Office information?

His hands were clammy and his back was wet as he made his way up in the lift and got out on the floor of his office. He made his way towards his desk without moving his eyes from it. The chair had been moved.

It was probably just the cleaners, he told himself. *No need to overreact.* They always came in the early hours of Tuesday morning, and this week would be no different.

Unable to control his urgency, he unlocked his machine and tapped in the password. The error message wasn't one he was expecting.

You have entered an incorrect password.

. . .

Swallowing hard, he tried again, his fingers dancing over the keyboard as he entered the password.

Again, the same error message.

Sam wiped the sweat from his brow and entered the password a third time, this time calming his trembling hands and entering the combination of letters, numbers and symbols slowly and carefully, before pressing Enter.

This time the machine popped back to life, taking him straight to the screen he'd been on when he locked the computer the night before: his data retrieval program.

There were hundreds of results on the screen, most of them partial matches or fragments of data which were completely irrelevant to Sam. After all, the data must have gone back years — and Sullivan wasn't exactly a rare name.

He scanned the results, noting a few which clearly referred to the future Prime Minister but in a purely professional and normal manner, before his eyes settled on one partial data fragment.

The sentence was far from complete, but it stood out like a sore thumb to Sam.

— s believed to share similar sexual proclivities to Michael Sullivan, Ba —

He performed a right-click on the fragment and asked the program to run its matching algorithm to see if any other data fragments had likely formed part of the same original document or file.

It returned one result. A result which left Sam breathless

and cold.

— *estigated, but never charged, in connection with Operation Cathedral into the Wonderland paedophile ring in 199 —*

35

Sam locked his computer, pushed back his chair and rose unsteadily to his feet before making his way towards the staff toilets.

As he left the open plan office, he felt a firm hand on his shoulder, stopping him dead in his tracks.

'Sam? What's wrong?' came the familiar and reassuring voice of Lucy. 'You look like you've seen a ghost.'

'Oh. Yeah. Not feeling too well, sorry.'

'Maybe you should go home. You've been through a lot recently. It can't be doing you any good.'

If only you knew the half of it, Sam thought. 'Nah, it's alright. I've got plenty to be getting on with here. It'll take my mind off things. It's better for me to be here, trust me.'

'Well, alright. But if you change your mind, you know I've always got your back, don't you?' Lucy said, placing a reassuring hand on his upper arm as she smiled warmly at him.

Sam forced his own smile and nodded, before heading into the toilets and retching into the sink.

. . .

Ten minutes later, having wiped the cold sweat from his face, Sam returned to his desk and sat down.

He stared at the computer screen for a full minute before taking a deep breath and unlocking his machine again.

He knew what the text on the screen said, but it was still as shocking as the first time he'd read it.

Wonderland seemed to ring a vague bell somewhere at the back of his mind, but he couldn't recall any details. The wording of the sentence didn't leave much to the imagination, though.

Paedophile ring.

He swallowed and steadied himself. He could only presume that —*estigated* had originally been 'investigated', but the key bit came after: *never charged*. That didn't mean Sullivan was innocent, of course, but it also far from confirmed his guilt.

He looked at the two fragments of text again.

— *s believed to share similar sexual proclivities to Michael Sullivan, Ba* —

— *estigated, but never charged, in connection with Operation Cathedral into the Wonderland paedophile ring in 1 9 9* —

There was too little to go on to confirm either way, but it was entirely possible the document didn't even refer to Sullivan. The first fragment seemed to suggest it was about somebody else — someone who shared 'similar sexual proclivities' to the man who was almost certain to be Britain's next Prime Minister.

There was nothing to suggest for certain that those sexual

proclivities involved a paedophile ring. Perhaps Sullivan and the person in question both enjoyed a bit of light bondage. Who knew? But Sam had an uneasy feeling.

First of all, why had this particular file been deleted? Who was being protected, if not Sullivan? And if all Sullivan and this mystery person shared was a penchant for handcuffs, why was the sentence worded to suggest that Sullivan was the benchmark of sexual deviancy, rather than the future PM sharing some similar proclivities to the mystery person? It seemed to suggest to Sam that Sullivan's own sexual deviancy was more extreme still.

And who had been investigated but not charged in connection with the investigation into the paedophile ring? Sullivan? The mystery person? Either way, Sullivan's name was inextricably linked, and Sam had to know why and how.

For the second time that morning, but this time feeling decidedly perkier, he locked his computer, stood up and walked towards the lift.

As he got close to it, he saw Lucy walking back through the office with a mug of hot coffee.

'Alright?' she said, smiling as she passed.

'Yeah, I think so. I will be, anyway. You were right, I'm not feeling brilliant. I'm going to go outside and get some fresh air for fifteen minutes.'

'You take your time,' she said, smiling. 'Some things are more important than work.'

Sam took the lift down to the ground floor and exited the building onto the street. He walked a hundred yards or so before stopping and leaning back against a wall.

He pulled his phone out of his pocket, made sure he was

connected to his phone network's own 4G signal, then loaded incognito mode on his mobile browser.

He typed *Wonderland paedophile ring* into the search bar and waited for the results to load.

They did so almost instantly.

The Wikipedia page for Operation Cathedral was the first one to appear, so he tapped to load it and took a minute to read the words on the screen in front of him.

A skim read told him Operation Cathedral was a major police operation conducted in the late 1990s across thirteen countries, spearheaded by the British National Crime Squad and staffed by 1,500 officers. It had broken up a major international child pornography ring called The Wonderland Club. The ring had been linked to the rape of an eight-year-old girl in the United States, as well as numerous other allegations of actual sexual assault and the sharing of child pornography.

The ring was believed to have had 180 members, six of whom ended their own lives after the raids had been conducted. 1,263 different children were exploited in the images. Only seventeen were ever identified, including a six-year-old from the United Kingdom and a seven-year-old from the United States.

The UK members of the Wonderland ring were jailed for between twelve and thirty months.

The fact that even the most serious offenders had only been sentenced for two and a half years sent shockwaves through the system, and raised questions as to why the Establishment and lawmakers deemed such light sentencing necessary. It also caused people to question who was looking out for their own interests, and whether the light sentencing was designed to ensure those jailed kept quiet about the more prominent members of the ring.

Even a public backlash ensured the maximum penalty was only increased to ten years, and it was believed amongst certain circles that the remaining Wonderland ring members were still in operation.

Sam locked his phone and put it back in his pocket, taking a deep lungful of London air. Was this the high-level governmental corruption The Firm had warned him about? Was this what they were alluding to?

He swallowed hard and headed back to the Home Office, riding the lift back to his floor and sitting back down at his desk.

He crossed his fingers and prayed the identity of the person who deleted the record would still be traceable. All digital activity left a footprint of some sort, and he just hoped there hadn't been enough rain to wash away this particular one since it had been left.

He was in luck.

There were only two pieces of information on the footprint: the name of the person who'd deleted the file, and the date on which it had been deleted.

The date was almost ten years ago, and only a few months before Sam had started working at the Home Office.

The name was Stephen Marwood.

36

By now, thoughts of leaving his own digital footprints were far from Sam's mind. He had something potentially huge within his grasp, and he needed to discover the truth.

He loaded the Home Office's intranet system and navigated his way to the staff directory. Each staff member was listed, alongside their official government email address, phone extension and work mobile phone number if they had one.

He typed Stephen Marwood's name into the search bar and pressed Enter.

No results.

His first thought was to go to a superior and ask if a Stephen Marwood had ever worked in the department, but that wasn't a great idea. Sam didn't know who he could trust, and he needed to limit the number of people he leaned on in order to gather information.

There was only one thing for it: good old detective work.

He took his laptop out of its bag — the only machine that would connect to the external internet from his office — and started it up before opening a web browser. He went straight to LinkedIn and searched for Stephen Marwood's name.

The first result showed a man of a similar age to Sam, living in Battersea, whose career history showed him working at the Home Office until just days before Sam started there. Had he been Stephen Marwood's replacement?

He opened another browser window alongside Marwood's LinkedIn page and loaded up Facebook. Again, he searched for the man's name, before scrolling down through the results to find a picture or location which matched the Stephen Marwood he'd found on LinkedIn.

There was nothing.

This wasn't something he was going to be able to do on his own. There was one person he knew who would have access to Home Office staff records. One person whose job was to oversee that sort of information. One person he knew — thought — he could trust.

Dee.

The office she worked in was a little busy for Sam's liking, but he couldn't exactly tell everyone else to leave, so he waited for a moment where it was as quiet as it'd ever be, then ambled over to her desk and sat down beside her.

'I need a huge favour,' he said.

'What sort of favour?'

'I need some information on a former Home Office employee. A guy who worked here just before me, same department.'

Dee raised her hand just a little, indicating that Sam should stop talking. She handed him a scrap of paper and a pen.

He looked at it, then back at her, then wrote the name *Stephen Marwood* on the paper.

Dee stared at the name for a moment, then opened up a screen on her computer and typed it in.

'Left just before you started,' she said.

'Does it say why?'

Dee took a deep breath and sighed. 'Yes and no,' she said. 'The termination code is classified. Beyond my pay grade to see it.'

'What, you can't see why he left?'

'Nope. There are a few different termination codes used. Resignation, redundancy, retirement, different levels of disciplinary termination... But this one means the reasons are classified.'

'And what does that mean?'

'It means someone doesn't want us to know why he left the Home Office.'

Frustrated, Sam knew there was only one thing for it. Not keen on the idea of making his way back down to the street again, he went into the toilets and locked himself in the only cubicle with an external window. Pushing the window open as far as it'd go — which wasn't far — he unpicked the stitching from the sole of his shoe and pulled out the SIM card he'd been given by The Firm.

He took his own personal SIM out of his phone and carefully inserted the new one, then stood on the toilet cistern and half-hung out of the window whilst he waited for the new SIM to connect.

It seemed to take an age, but when it finally connected to the network, he opened up his Contacts list and scrolled down the short list to *DATA*. He selected *Send Message* and tapped out a text.

. . .

Need address and info on Stephen Marwood, possibly resident in Battersea. Ex HO.

He pressed *Send* and the phone informed him the message had been delivered immediately and read barely three seconds later.

He waited anxiously for a reply for what seemed like hours, but when he finally saw the on-screen ellipsis which indicated a response was being composed, he held his breath and watched the screen.

Then the reply came.

He had an address.

37

Sam's heart was pounding and he could feel damp patches under his armpits as he exited the toilet and stood in the corridor, unsure which way to turn.

'We need to stop meeting like this,' came the voice of Lucy, cheerful as ever. 'You've not been ill again, have you?'

Sam blinked hard. 'Uh, yeah. Not feeling great. Sorry.'

'Seriously, Sam. Go home. You need to rest. Forget everything else, alright?'

He took a deep breath and nodded. 'Yeah. Yeah, you're right. I'll grab my stuff and go.'

Lucy placed a reassuring hand on his arm. 'Good idea. Don't come back until you feel better, either. Sometimes you've got to look after number one.' She planted a kiss on his cheek. 'Stay safe.'

There was no truly anonymous way to travel in London, but Sam reckoned a taxi was about the closest one could get.

The journey took a little over twenty-five minutes, the traffic heavy throughout central London and around the river.

As far as Sam was concerned, there was no time to waste. He wasn't the sort of person who thought about doing something then spent weeks or months thinking about it even more. He was a doer, and that meant getting on with things as soon as the decision had been made.

And it was that personality trait which led him to stand at the entrance to Stephen Marwood's block of flats a little over half an hour after being given the address.

He pressed the intercom buzzer for flat 9, and waited a few moments for Marwood to pick up.

There was nothing.

Sam tried again, waiting a full thirty seconds this time before concluding that Marwood probably wasn't in. He'd try again another time.

As he turned to leave, a middle-aged man in a dark Harrington jacket pressed the blank button in the bottom-right-hand corner of the keypad, unlocking the front door.

'Tradesman's entrance,' he said, his accent reminiscent of the north east.

Sam nodded his thanks, and walked through the now-unlocked front door to the flats. He jogged up the stairs until he reached flat 9, then froze.

The door was ajar.

Sam edged his way forward towards the door and nudged it open with his foot. There was silence inside.

'Hello?' he called, cautiously at first.

Nothing.

His senses on high alert, Sam stepped into the flat, looking behind him as he did so. There didn't seem to be anyone around.

He pushed open a door on his right, and saw the gleaming white kitchen tiles appear into view. As the door swung further open, his view of the tiles was interrupted by something altogether different — a man hanging from the ceiling, his face blue, his arms dangling by his side as his head settled at an unnatural angle.

Without thinking, Sam picked up the wooden chair that was lying on its side beneath the man, grabbed a serrated knife from the knife block, climbed up and cut the cord from which the man was suspended.

The man fell to the floor with a sickening thud, but still did not move.

Sam jumped down from the chair and felt the man's pulse. There was nothing, but he was still warm.

Trying desperately to remember what he could from his minimal first aid training, he performed chest compressions and mouth-to-mouth resuscitation on the man he presumed to be Stephen Marwood, but he knew instinctively there was no point.

The man was dead.

Sam ran back out of the flat and cleared the stairs three at a time, pushing open the front door back onto the street. He looked in both directions, desperate to find someone to ask for help but finding for the first time in his life that the streets of London seemed strangely desolate.

Just as he was about to head back into the building, movement caught Sam's eye on the other side of the street. A man

was standing on the other side of a black BMW saloon, next to
the open front passenger's door.

It was the Geordie who'd let him into the building just a few
minutes earlier. He locked eyes with Sam for a few moments,
his face impassive. Performing one slow, slight nod, the man
climbed into the passenger seat, closed his door and the car
pulled away.

38

Sam didn't return home until many hours later that night. He'd walked around in a daze for a while, his brain overwhelmed with everything that had happened over the past few days and weeks.

Stephen Marwood had been complicit in deleting records of the future Prime Minister's potential involvement in a paedophile ring, and had subsequently lost his job at the Home Office, ultimately being replaced by Sam. Marwood had lived without any problem for a good few years since, but within minutes of Sam discovering his identity and looking him up, Marwood was dead.

And who was the man in the BMW? He'd spoken to Sam, let him into the flats. Where had he come from and where did he go? He'd appeared at Sam's side, and he didn't think the man had followed him into the building. Now he thought about it, that was a little odd but he hadn't thought much of it at the time. Was he the man who'd killed Stephen Marwood?

That then begged the question as to how these people had been tipped off that Sam had been looking into Marwood. They hadn't had much time — maybe an hour at the most since he'd first discovered the man's name himself — which was a ridiculously quick window in which to act. For how long had they been waiting to pounce? Was it his internet searches that tipped them off? If so, someone was monitoring his smartphone. Was it the search Dee had performed on the personnel database? That would have given them even less time to act. Or could it have been Dee herself?

The thought was mindboggling. Sam had only just come to terms with the fact that Dee had been a secret member of The Firm, without trying to get his head around the possibility that she was actually working for a darker force. Or was The Firm the dark force behind the murder of Stephen Marwood? It wasn't too much of a flight of fancy to consider. After all, he knew very little about The Firm and had trusted their good intentions purely because Dee and Jason were involved. What if they, too, were a rogue organisation and Sam had been roped in as some sort of fall guy or asset to be used and disposed of?

Most worryingly of all, it led him to the unsettling realisation that his survival of the Westminster Underground bombing might not have been entirely intended. Was he meant to die that day? Had he inadvertently got too close to a truth he didn't even know had existed? He couldn't see how — he hadn't known any of this even existed until Jason's unsolicited approach in the hospital — but to Sam every possibility seemed both more plausible and less fantastic than the last. He was starting to believe that anything was possible.

His mind numb, he'd wandered the residential streets of Battersea before ending up at Clapham Junction station. With no particular destination in mind, he got onto the Overground service and headed north, crossing the river and passing through the palatial suburbs of west London, his mind elsewhere as the train rattled along the tracks, stopping every few minutes.

As the train pulled away from Kensal Rise station, he realised he was now in unfamiliar territory in north London. Unfamiliar, but strangely comforting. He didn't want to be in south London, and he certainly didn't want to be in the centre of town. Glancing at the line map above the seats in front of him, he spotted the name of a station he'd alighted at some months previously for a friend's birthday drinks — Gospel Oak. It was home to a pub Sam had never been into before, but which he'd immediately found to be both charming and fascinating.

The Southampton Arms was only a short walk from the station, but the moment he was inside he felt safe, transported back to a bygone age of spit and sawdust. The pub sold only real ales and ciders, and stocked pork pies and scotch eggs from a glass-fronted meat counter. There was no pretension here — no desire to capture the stockbrokers or bankers that the central London wine bars had courted. This was a proper old-school boozer with an open fire and the only source of music being an old-fashioned record player behind the bar, beside which sat a stack of jazz records on warm, fuzzy vinyl.

This was the Britain Sam remembered. This wasn't the sort of place terrorists visited. This wasn't the home of spies and conspiracies. This was comfortable. This was home. This was Britain.

39

Sam's head was swimming as he left the comfort of the Southampton Arms.

He'd decided to get an Uber home, despite the fact it had cost him over forty pounds. In retrospect, his Oyster card seemed like a bargain — and would probably have got him home quicker — but he didn't feel in any state of mind to brave public transport.

The alcohol had done its job in dulling his senses, but the fresh air had given him a new clarity, purpose and anxiety as he tried — and failed — to get his head around recent events.

It was now clear to Sam that the level of corruption was not only far more serious than he'd first assumed, but that it also went a lot higher. He didn't have the mental capacity to consider the internal machinations of what had happened, but he knew someone somewhere along the line had betrayed him. He was being watched. His actions were being observed. Someone was trying to send him a warning.

And it was working.

Because of his actions, because of having simply tried to find out some more information as to why an employee had left the Home Office, a man was now dead. How far were these people willing to go to protect their secrets and stop the truth from coming out? Who were they? And what was the truth?

The more Sam thought about it, the more anxious he became. He was in well over his head here, and if it hadn't been for the copious amounts of alcohol he'd been drinking, there was no way he would have been approaching Dee's home with the intention of calling her out on it.

Dee seemed genuinely surprised to see Sam standing on her doorstep, and Sam felt a small pang of guilt at having knocked so late.

'I was just heading to bed. What's up?'

'I think I'd better come in,' Sam said, trying to sound sober. 'If you're alone, that is.'

Dee looked at him for a moment. 'Yes,' she said, 'I am,' and stepped aside to let him in.

'Who did it?' Sam asked, standing in her hallway.

'Did what?'

'You know what.'

'Have you been drinking?'

'Don't change the subject, Dee. Who killed Stephen Marwood?'

Dee froze, her eyes turning glassy and her breath shallow.

'What?' she whispered.

'You heard.'

'He's dead?'

'I found him swinging from his kitchen ceiling. Still warm.'

'When?'

'Today. About half an hour after I mentioned his name to you.'

Dee blinked a few times. 'What, and you think I had something to do with that?'

'Well it's a bit of a fucking coincidence, isn't it?' Sam said, raising his voice.

'No, of course it bloody isn't. But that doesn't mean I had anything to do with it. Who else did you tell?'

'No-one.'

'Someone's watching us. How did you get his address?'

'Data.'

Dee shook her head. 'There won't be a leak there. You contacted him from your Firm SIM?'

'Of course I fucking did. I'm not stupid.'

'In your own handset?'

'Yeah. I was at work.'

Dee scraped back her hair. 'It's possible the handset's been compromised. That means Data has been too. We'll have to get word to Travers. He'll need to organise a clean-up at Marwood's flat, too. Your fingerprints and DNA will be all over it.'

'Fuck Travers, Dee. Fuck the SIM card. Are you even listening to what I'm saying? Stephen Marwood was the last person we know had access to records which linked Michael Sullivan to a child sex gang. Less than an hour after we discover that, he's dead. Do you see what we're dealing with here?'

'Sam, calm down,' Dee said, putting a hand on his shoulder, quickly finding it shrugged off. 'Look, this is what we've been trying to tell you. We're dealing with some serious stuff here. These people do not mess around. If something is in their way, or if someone might threaten their secrets, they'll do whatever it takes.'

'But how? I don't get how.'

'Me neither. They've got links everywhere. The corruption's in government, the police, the army, the newspapers, the media owners, big business, everywhere. It's all interlinked, everyone looking out for each other's interests, keeping their world separate from ours. It's money, Sam. Money talks. But fortunately not everyone with money is evil. There are plenty who don't play these games. And they're the people who fund us.'

Sam let out a small laugh, and shook his head. 'So the people who weren't in the game, and didn't like the game, decided to set up their own game designed to ruin the other one? And that makes them better how?'

'Because we don't go around killing people or exploiting the public for our own gain. We're the ones keeping them in check.'

'And how am I meant to know that? I don't know what's what right now, Dee. Have you ever seen that comedy sketch where the two military guys question whether they might be the baddies? Because that's the point, isn't it? Everyone thinks they're the good guys and the other side are the bad guys. Sullivan and his lot probably don't think they're doing anything wrong, either. He probably thinks we're the bad guys for trying to disrupt his career and blacken his name. What *is* right, Dee?'

Dee leaned back against the wall, her arms folded across her chest. 'That's a question you have to ask yourself, Sam. I can't tell you how to think. But all I know at the moment is you're not thinking straight. You're jumping about all over the place.'

'What the hell do you expect?'

'Sam, calm down. Please. We're on the same side here.'

'Are we? Are we really? Because the only person I told about Stephen Marwood was you. And half an hour later the guy's dead. Are you still going to tell me we're on the same side?'

Dee sighed. 'Sam, why are you here? Are you here to tell me

about Marwood or to accuse me of having him killed? Make your mind up.'

'I don't know! I don't know anything any more,' Sam said, sliding down the wall until his backside was on the floor, his knees pulled up to his chest. He didn't suspect Dee. Not really. At least, he didn't think he did. It was her face when he told her about Marwood's death — the stunned silence — that had convinced him she hadn't known. But in that look there was something else. Something which told Sam she'd had a sudden realisation about something. If he felt further from the truth than ever before, he had a growing feeling that Dee was now one step closer.

40

The next morning's hangover didn't seem to make the previous night's excesses worth it, as far as Sam was concerned. However, he was well aware it was something he'd needed at the time.

For the first night in a long time, he had actually slept the whole way through. The amount of alcohol he'd drunk meant it wasn't the best sleep he'd ever had, though, and he woke up feeling more tired than when he'd gone to bed.

He'd barely been awake a minute before the thoughts and questions started flooding back into his mind, making him wish he'd never woken up in the first place. Marwood's death made perfect sense, but at the same time absolutely no sense at all.

It was clear Sam had uncovered something, and was close to discovering the truth. The speed with which they'd reacted in seeing off Marwood had made that clear. But why now? If Marwood had known the truth for years, why wasn't he silenced earlier? What had led them to believe he would talk to Sam? And why hadn't they killed Sam instead? After all, he was the one delving into their secrets and actively trying to discover the truth. Marwood was no more of a threat than he had been over the past few years.

None of it made any sense.

His head pounding, he reached into his bedside drawer unit for some paracetamol and downed the pint of water from the glass next to him. His plan to take a few days off work wasn't going to happen. He couldn't sit around at home doing nothing, going stir crazy, especially now he knew there were some seriously dark forces at play.

Had he intended to go back to work the next day, there was no way he would have drunk as much as he did the previous night, but this was no time for Sam to feel sorry for himself. He had plenty to be getting on with.

His stomach was still churning, so he decided to forego breakfast and instead took a hot shower, got dressed, picked up his laptop bag and headed into work as if it was any other day.

The noise and lights seemed louder and brighter than they usually did, and Sam wondered whether he might've still been drunk. He hoped the 'fresh' air of London's streets might help clear that.

He stopped at a pedestrian crossing and adjusted his laptop bag on his shoulder as he took deep lungfuls of air and waited for the lights to change. As he did so, he became aware of a moped approaching from his right-hand side. Before he'd realised the bike was actually driving along the pavement, he felt a hard tug pulling him to the ground, a sharp pain shooting through his shoulder as he looked up and saw the two men swerving back onto the road and riding away, clutching his laptop bag.

'Shit!'

Sam watched as the other Londoners took note of the

changing lights and started to cross the road, ignoring his plight. There were times when he hated this poxy city.

He got to his feet, pushing himself up with his good arm, then took his phone out of his pocket and dialled Dee with shaking hands.

'Dee. Fuck, I've just been mugged.'

'What? Where? What happened?'

'On my way to work. Two guys on a moped, they nicked my laptop bag and rode off.'

'What was in the bag?'

'Just my laptop.'

'Nothing else?'

'No.'

'Right. We'll wipe it remotely. There won't be anything left on it, don't worry.'

'What? How can you do that?'

'Don't ask. More to the point, are you okay?'

'Shoulder's stuffed. Bit shaken. But that might just be the DTs.'

'Well get yourself in the office sharpish. We'll clean you up.'

Sam ended the call, feeling both reassured and even more deeply concerned at the same time.

41

'Did you get a good look at them?' Dee asked, dabbing the graze on Sam's arm with antiseptic. She'd met Sam at the front desk and had taken him straight through into a disused office space, where they'd be free from prying eyes.

'No, they both had helmets on. Black jackets, black trousers. Not a chance.'

'Number plate?'

'Didn't even think to look. There might not have been one.'

'We'll get CCTV checked. At the very least we'll be able to trace them back and find out where they first appeared. Not that it'd be a massive surprise even if we did manage to trace them back to their employer. They'll only be bottom rung, anyway, paid off cheaply to nick your bag and give it to someone else. They probably didn't even know your name.'

'Yeah, that makes me feel loads better,' Sam said. 'Thanks.'

'This isn't about you, Sam. No matter how much it might feel like it is. You're just a pawn in this game.'

'For them or for you?'

'For everyone.'

'Wow, thanks. Way to make me feel valued.'

'Even pawns are valued. There's always one that breaks free at the front and promotes itself to a higher rank.'

Sam scoffed. 'If that's meant to be some sort of analogy about me, I'm afraid you've lost me.'

'Like I said, Barker. It's not all about you.'

'Yeah, well maybe none of it should be about me. I've had enough.'

Dee looked at him, but said nothing. No words were needed.

After a few moments, she sat back and said, 'I understand why you might feel that way, Sam, but you can't back out now. That's why they're doing what they're doing. They didn't want what was on that laptop. They knew we could wipe it remotely and leave no trace of anything. They're not stupid. Taking it was symbolic. It was to let you know they knew. The laptop was a symbol of the great work you've been doing.'

'Yeah, well I don't really fancy being attacked on my way to work, no matter how symbolic. Nor do I fancy putting more people's lives in danger just to play some stupid game of spies.'

Dee sighed and leaned forward.

'Sam, far more lives will be put in danger if we don't stick with this. There will be more attacks. More bombings. More reactionary events. People will die in the streets. In their homes. On their way to school. And if this rising tide sweeps Sullivan into number ten, who knows what the result will be? Deportations. State-sponsored attacks. Public beheadings? Nothing is too fanciful right now. We're going down a long, dark path.'

'Yeah, well you can't blame me for what terrorists do. They'll carry on regardless, and that's one ethos of theirs I'm willing to subscribe to. I want to go back to my old, boring life where nothing happened and no-one wanted to kill me. Keep calm and carry on. What those bastards do is nothing to do with me.'

'But it is, Sam. What about Benji and Leila?'

Sam swallowed hard. 'You leave them out of this.'

'It's not that simple, Sam. You've seen the retaliatory attacks on Muslims. It could be them next.'

'They're not Muslims.'

'Oh for Christ's sake, Sam, their surname is Mohammed. Two bloody Hindus were beaten up in London recently just for being a bit brown. What difference do you think it's going to make to a knuckle-dragging skinhead that Leila ditched her religion in her teenage years? And your son's hardly taken on your skin colour genes, has he?'

Sam clenched his teeth and tried not to let his feelings show. He'd never considered Leila or Benji to be Muslims. They weren't. Leila had renounced Islam before going to university, and by the time Sam met her she showed no signs of the girl who'd been brought up in a British Muslim household. The thought that a rising tide of anti-Islamic violence might affect his own family was almost unbearable. Living in a major city — even one as tolerant and forward-thinking as Edinburgh — would magnify that risk enormously.

'Sam, we are dealing with some fucked up people here. That Wonderland link could bring down Sullivan, but we need more. It ties in with some things we thought we already knew.'

'Like what?'

Dee looked around furtively. 'Let's just say it wasn't a massive surprise when you told me what you'd found. There were rumours a while back that Sullivan had been involved in some sort of sex ring. There was a girl who went to the police and told them a group of men had raped her at the old Smith-field Aerodrome. It was hushed up. The girl was made out to be a liar. Her parents tried going to the papers, and somehow that got back to the top brass. Twenty-four hours later, dad dies in a car accident. Hit and run. The other driver was never found. This is what we're dealing with here.'

Sam shook his head. 'It's not something I want to get involved with. This is beyond my pay grade, Dee.'

'You're just a cog in the machine, Sam. But all cogs are vital. Lose one, and the whole machine breaks down. Yes, they tried to scare you. And they did it so you'd back off. The moment you show them it's worked, it's game over. You're a Londoner. You know all about standing tall in the face of adversity and carrying on regardless.'

'I'm also sick to the back teeth of people telling me what I am and what I should do.'

Dee forced a sympathetic smile. 'No-one's telling you anything, Sam. All I can do is try to help. It's entirely up to you whether you want to accept that help. The ball's in your court.'

WORLD'S LARGEST 3D PRINTED OBJECT TO COMMEMORATE VICTIMS OF WESTMINSTER BOMBING

The world's largest 3D printed object is to be unveiled as a fitting memorial to the victims of the Westminster bombing.

The piece has been designed by up-and-coming Muslim artist Khalid Saleem and funded by wealthy British Muslim businessman Mohammad Yousuf Zaher as an expression of peace between the Muslim and white British communities.

The work, entitled 'One', incorporates a peace dove surrounded by thirty-two people — one for each London borough — holding hands.

Saleem, 26, of Ealing, said, 'I wanted to create something that would show unity between the Muslim community and the white British community. London will not be divided by terrorists, nor by reactionary nationalist extremism. We are a city founded on peace and togetherness.'

Zaher, whose business empire includes hotels, golf clubs and private hedge funds, said it was 'important that people see London is not divided, but more united than ever.' He added: 'The concept of creating this piece as the world's largest 3D printed object is, I think, revolutionary. It would have been easy to commission a bronze statue or stone monument, but this shows forward thinking and a way of doing something differently, rather than simply carrying on as we always have done. I think that's a message which resonates.'

The piece will be unveiled in Parliament Square Garden next week.

The next couple of days passed with relative ease and quiet for Sam. Dee had, thankfully, given him some time and space to get his head straight in the wake of everything that had happened. Sam felt no closer to a decision, but he appreciated the distance all the same.

Recent events had played havoc with his anxiety. It would be enough to make anyone anxious, but Sam was already prone and susceptible. He wondered whether that was one of the reasons The Firm had apparently been monitoring him for so long and whether that was why they'd not approached him sooner. Not that he was thanking them for approaching him now.

How far did their reach extend? Did they know his medical history? Probably. For all he knew, they had cameras and microphones in his flat and had witnessed every panic attack or mini episode of anxiety before opening his front door.

It was something he'd largely learned to manage and live with, and he was well aware it was something he'd probably never be completely rid of.

Going to work was something he'd always found easy in comparison to most social situations. It was something he knew. The pattern was familiar. He'd go to the same café for his breakfast, take the same route to work — sometimes on a good day he'd push himself by taking a slight detour — and perform more or less the same tasks while he was there. It was comfortable. And on his darkest days he'd remind himself just how impressive it was that he still managed to make that journey, still managed to complete a day's work, all because he'd pushed himself into that routine.

He knew the moment he took a day off work in the face of extreme anxiety, it would win. And he wondered if his time off in the wake of the Westminster bombing was one of the reasons why it was now starting to take over more and more. Not that he needed any more reasons to feel anxious right now.

Once again, he forced himself out of bed, showered, got dressed and headed into work.

He walked into the familiar office, the smells, sights and sounds all as he knew them to be.

'Sam? You got a sec?' called Frank, his immediate boss. There was something in his tone that Sam didn't like. Not one bit.

He followed Frank through into his office, closing the door behind him.

Frank sat down behind his desk and gestured for Sam to take a seat.

'Sam, I'm going to be honest. This is a bit of an awkward conversation to be having,' Frank said, leaving Sam wondering where this was going. 'I've had word from above that the minister has decided priorities are changing. Sullivan's putting a hell of a lot of pressure on domestic security in the wake of the

Westminster bomb, and the minister is responding by diverting more Home Office funds towards counter-terrorism operations.'

Sam blinked a few times, and nodded slowly. 'Right. Well that's a good thing, surely?'

Frank took a deep breath. 'In the greater scheme of things, yes.'

'But?'

'But resources are finite. We've been told we have to cut some administrative roles and slim down our staffing in some of the less... active... departments. That includes us.'

'You're cutting staff?' Sam asked.

'Unfortunately so.'

'How many?' Sam asked, swallowing.

'I'm afraid I'm not at liberty to divulge that.'

'But I'm one of them, right?'

'That's correct.'

Even though Sam had known for a few seconds what was coming, Frank's words still hit him like a crossbow bolt through the chest. All he could do was slowly nod.

'I realise it's probably a bit of a shock to you, Sam, but my hands are tied.'

'Right. When?'

'The minister has demanded the funding be shifted to counter-terrorism immediately. He's had orders from the prime minister. The election won't be far off, and he needs to be seen to be taking firm action as quickly as possible.'

'How quickly?'

'Like I said. Immediately.'

'Right. So my notice period starts now?'

'Not exactly,' Frank said, leaning back in his chair. 'Your notice period will be paid in full, but departing IT staff are seen as a security risk, especially considering the access and privileges you have. You'll be placed on immediate gardening leave.'

'Gardening leave?'

'It's standard protocol when someone has access to the Home Office's IT systems. There's too much at risk. You know the threats and dangers we're dealing with at the moment, Sam.'

There was something in the way Frank said those words which gave Sam the impression they were somehow barbed or double-edged.

'We can get you someone to help clear your desk, if you like.'

Sam looked at Frank, unable even to process the words he was hearing, never mind decipher any potential double meaning or implied threat.

Instead, he stood quietly and pushed his chair in, angry, betrayed and devastated on the inside, but the same calm, quiet and gentle Sam Barker everyone else saw on the outside.

43

Although he visited the pub regularly in order to force himself to fight his social anxiety, Sam had never considered himself to be a drinker. Despite this, he'd made sure to pick up two bottles of the cheapest whisky he could find in the corner shop on his way home, with the full intention of drinking as much of it as he could before he was violently sick.

Between the shop and his flat, he decided to call Dee. He'd been subjected to the ignominy of having security staff stand over him while he cleared his desk of any personal effects, before escorting him to the entrance to the building, stripping him of his security clearance and leaving him out on the street.

Sam had never felt so humiliated in his life. He felt sure there was more behind it than simple budget cuts. He'd seen plenty of budget cuts before, especially in the wake of the global financial crisis and the swingeing cuts the government had brought in following that. He couldn't remember ever witnessing anyone being physically escorted off the premises because of that.

And there had been something in Frank's tone, too. Something threatening. Was this because of the program he'd written and run on their servers? If so, why didn't they just say that? Surely they had to tell him the real reason for his dismissal, otherwise he'd be able to drag them through the courts. None of it made any sense.

Fortunately for him, Dee answered her mobile phone quickly.

'You're not going to believe this,' he said. 'I've been sacked.'

'Wrong on both counts,' Dee replied, the calm voice of reason. 'They won't have sacked you. That would mean drawing attention to what you were investigating. They'll have made you redundant and used some shitty excuse to push it through. And yes, I totally believe it. I had a feeling they might try pulling a stunt like this.'

'Who? Sullivan's not in control of the Home Office. He's not prime minister yet.'

'Oh Sam, you've got a lot to learn. The prime minister controls very little. That's not where the power lies. And he's certainly not in control of the Home Office. Trust me, when they told you they were making you redundant it wasn't the Home Office speaking. It was Sullivan.'

'What, so now you're telling me Frank is on Sullivan's payroll?'

'Be careful what you say on the phone, Sam.'

Even though he knew Dee wasn't at work today and couldn't be physically overheard, she was right: there was no way of knowing if one of their phones had been bugged.

'Listen, meet me in the last public place you saw me. We'll talk there,' Sam replied, before putting down the phone.

44

Sam got to the Barley Mow a few minutes before Dee, and ordered two pints of London Pride. Right now, Sam had nothing to feel proud of — particularly not when it came to the capital of his homeland, which had completely let him down in recent days — but the running joke was one he couldn't avoid.

Jokes in general were far from Sam's mind as he sat down in a booth and waited for Dee, who arrived looking as calm and unflustered as ever.

'Sam, I'm sorry,' she said, placing a hand on his.

'Don't be. I didn't think for one moment that decision came from HR. Did you really not get word of it until I told you?'

Dee shook her head. 'No. That in itself is probably a warning to me. Cutting me out of the loop isn't something they'd normally do.'

'If they know, why not just get rid of you too?'

'Better the devil you know, Sam. They know lots of things about lots of people. They aren't stupid. They know they've got a chance of getting much more out of it if they just sit and watch. I know they're there. I know they're watching me. But they're after the big guns. We're just pawns in the game. They're happy to let us scurry around, hopefully leading them to the people they really want.'

'How the hell can you live like that?' Sam asked. 'It's messing me up as it is.'

'You get used to it. I've been doing it long enough. As I say, it's all part of the game.'

'Yeah, well it doesn't feel much like a game to me.'

'Trust me, Sam. You don't know the half of it. How are you feeling?'

'Upset. Angry. Betrayed. Like I want to hurt someone.'

'Probably best you don't do that.'

'No, but I need to do something. This isn't right, Dee. This isn't justice. We can't let those bastards get away with it.'

'You don't need to.'

'And what use am I to you now? There was very little I was able to do as it was, apart from harvest data from a few servers. I fail to see what I can do now I'm not even allowed in the poxy building.'

Dee stayed silent for a few moments. 'Do you need to be in the building?'

Sam looked at her, the cogs starting to turn in his head.

'How do you mean?'

'Surely it would have been far less risky anyway if you were to create what you need to create from home, then use someone on the inside to run it on the local servers.'

'Well thanks for shutting the stable door after the horse has bolted, Dee.'

'You know what I mean, Sam. Think about it. I still have access to the building.'

'But not the servers.'

Dee sat back against the back of the booth, exhaling. 'Good point. Is there a way of me getting access to them?'

Sam shook his head. 'We can't trust anyone else in there. We don't know who's behind this or who's on Sullivan's payroll. If they're getting rid of anyone who's not on side, it stands to reason that there's more than one person who is.'

'What about security flaws or holes? Is there any potential way in?'

Sam let out a small involuntary laugh. 'You're talking to the man who used to plug them.'

It had been part of Sam's job to write code for the Home Office's servers whenever a security flaw was identified, and he knew better than most how the systems worked. There was no point at which the internal network could even remotely possibly be accessed from outside the Home Office, apart from a small technical window during maintenance restarts.

'Hang on,' Sam said, the realisation hitting him. 'Let me think this through. The servers undergo regular self-maintenance on a fortnightly basis. After the usual nightly backups, once a month they go through a sort of defragmentation and update process, applying any minor patches, that sort of thing. Once they're doing doing that, they restart, one at a time. When each one comes back online, there's a tiny window — probably only about two or three seconds at most — before the firewall and internal security takes hold. Technically — and I honestly have no idea if this would work — that's the one time where there might be a way in.'

'When's the next maintenance run?' Dee asked, all ears.

'Tomorrow night.'

'Shit. That'd be the last one until after the election, right?'

'Right.'

'What needs doing?'

'Well, I'd need to code a program first. Something which would create a network bridge that'd allow me to access the servers from outside. It's so risky, Dee. I'll tell you that much. I'm going to have to spoof privileges at a server level and open up an outside link that the firewall could spot at any time. My only advantage is being able to switch it on before the firewall comes back online, and hopefully convincing it to whitelist my connection.'

'Hopefully? Sam, you know the way those servers work better than anyone. It's your job.'

'*Was* my job. And it's easy enough when you've got them there in front of you and you can try it all out live. But coding a program for a system I can't even see or test on? I'd be doing this in the dark. It's like asking Da Vinci to paint the Mona Lisa blindfolded.'

'But it's possible?' Dee asked.

'Technically. Possibly. But I'd need your help.'

45

There was no denying it was a huge risk. His plan would put Dee right in the firing line and, if she was caught, would prove beyond any doubt that she was involved with The Firm.

There was also a slight issue in that Dee was not as technically minded as Sam. He'd have to show her exactly what needed doing, and when. The timing was crucial. There was a window of two, maybe three seconds. There was so much that could go wrong.

If they were successful, it would give Sam full remote access to the servers and all of the information on them. For that to happen, it would need Dee to run Sam's new code within that two to three second window before the server security kicked in. And even if she managed it, there was no guarantee the code would even work. There was no opportunity for testing. If it failed, the attempted security breach would be flagged up immediately, and Sam and Dee's digital fingerprints would be all over it.

Attempting to hack government computers wasn't exactly a petty crime. Sam would almost certainly receive a hefty prison sentence. The future prime minister — and likely current prime minister at the time of Sam's theoretical trial — would ensure they threw the book at him. And that's if he was lucky. Sam had already seen what Sullivan's people did to those who threatened their secrets.

Putting Dee at risk was something else which sat extremely uneasily with Sam. But what choice did he have? He no longer had access to the building, and there wasn't anyone else he knew he could trust. He was pretty sure Lucy was fine, but there was an element of doubt about everyone in Sam's mind now. At least with Dee, he knew she was in The Firm.

Besides which, the risks involved with not doing something were even higher. Seeing what had happened to Stephen Marwood had shown Sam exactly what these people were capable of. Until then, a large part of him had wondered how much of what Dee and Jason had told him could be true. Much of it sounded like a bizarre conspiracy theory. But wasn't that all part of the plan? The more outrageously they behaved, the less likely it was that anyone would believe them. And the more normalised that behaviour became, the more likely it was they'd get away with one step worse next time.

Dee had been willing to take the risk. That had been a great help to Sam in making his decision. If he'd had to talk her round, he didn't think he could have done it. The fact she needed no convincing and was more than willing to put herself in the firing line had told him a lot about her — but nothing he didn't already know deep down.

She was loyal. She was committed. She was always willing to go the extra mile if needed to. And those were the qualities that had attracted Sam to her over the years. She was a rock, providing him with surety and stability.

Of course, that had changed recently. Their dynamic was now different. And she'd introduced him to a world which had given him the polar opposites of surety and stability. It had rocked his world, turned it upside down. But Sam was starting to realise that he could barely reconcile his new world with the old. Things hadn't just changed; they were irreversible. His world had changed and he was going to have to change with it.

He'd thought of nothing else since coming up with the plan, and had tried not to think too much about its ramifications. He'd knuckled down, focusing on the task in hand and on writing the code the program needed.

It was multi-layered. The first layer of code tried to ensure the firewalls and security systems didn't spot it as a threat. This should have been fairly straightforward, seeing as they were systems Sam knew intricately and which he'd played a major part in coding. But there was no telling what measures had been taken on that front since he'd been dismissed.

The second layer would open up the connection to the external network, creating the first bridge between the outside world and the server.

The third layer would attempt to mask that bridge, making it more difficult for anyone to view that particular network traffic.

There was no denying it was ambitious. But as Sam spent more tired hours at his laptop, a huge flask of coffee next to him as he coded long into the night, he became more and more confident that they might just be able to pull this off.

46

Sam was woken from his sleep by a knocking at his front door. He pulled himself up, blinked hard and staggered over to the front door, opening it.

It was Jason Collins.

'Jason. Come in,' Sam said, standing aside.

'Afternoon kip?' Jason asked.

'Something like that. I've been working through the night. Kind of losing focus a bit now.'

'Well you make sure you don't burn yourself out. You won't be any good to anyone then,' his friend replied, placing a hand on his shoulder.

'Is that you talking as a friend or a colleague?'

Jason smiled. 'Both.'

'In that case, I appreciate your personal concern, but I'm afraid my line manager is Dee. Am I going to have to take this abuse of power up with my union?'

Jason laughed and patted Sam on the back. 'Behave yourself. Where's the coffee machine?'

Sam nodded his head in the direction of the small kitchen and followed Jason through.

'So what's the visit in aid of? You don't usually drop in unannounced. You don't usually drop in announced, come to think of it.'

'Just passing. Thought it might be wise to check you were still alive and well.'

'I'm alive,' Sam replied.

'Not a bad start, I suppose. Any luck?'

Sam realised in that moment that Jason knew about his and Dee's plan. Of course he did. Why wouldn't he?

'Yeah. I think we're just about there, actually. Just got to tidy up a few loose ends and compile, and I'm about as confident as I'll ever be.'

'And how confident is that, objectively speaking?'

Sam shrugged. 'Impossible to say. It's a bit like designing and building a plane from scratch in your own garage and sending it up full of passengers before you've even tested it. In theory, it works. But theory never killed anyone.'

'No-one will die, Sam.'

'Not immediately, no.'

Jason looked at Sam, and both men seemed to have an implicit understanding of what was at stake here. The risks were huge. But the potential rewards were even greater. The chance to bring down Sullivan once and for all — and to smash a hole in the Establishment corruption which threatened to plague Britain — was too much to resist.

'Did you see the news about the Westminster memorial?' Jason asked.

'Uh, I think I heard something. 3D printed, isn't it?'

'That's the one. They're unveiling it tomorrow. You going?'

'Why would I want to do that?' Sam asked, his eyes narrowing.

Jason shrugged. 'Same reason as everyone else, I suppose. Proud Londoner. Proud Briton. Plus you actually survived the attack. Going to be interesting to see how the mood changes afterwards, if we manage to pull off your little job.'

'I don't think it's my kind of thing,' Sam said.

'What, leaving the house? Socialising with strangers?'

Sam swallowed. He didn't see any problem with preferring his own company, and he certainly didn't see why Jason had to tease and revel in his anxiety.

'I can watch it on the telly. It doesn't make me any less of a Londoner if I don't turn up to every event in the city, Jason.'

Jason raised his hands in mock surrender. 'Alright, alright. Just thought you might fancy it.'

'Are you going?'

'No can do. Travers and I are off to Morocco this evening.'

'Romantic getaway?'

'Something like that. There are some very rich people over there who're being stifled by their system of government. Let's just call it official business and leave it at that.'

'Yeah, let's. I don't want to know.'

'It's all for the greater good, Sam.'

'Isn't that what all sides say?'

Jason smiled. 'You've played this game before.'

'I've been in the civil service long enough to realise changing the colour of a rosette doesn't mean a thing.'

'We are doing the right thing, though, Sam,' Jason said, placing a hand on his shoulder again and leaning in to him. 'We have to play the bastards at their own game, but we never — never — have blood on our hands. This is all about levelling the playing field. It's about making sure the truth gets out there, no matter how awkward or uncomfortable it is. No seediness, no corruption, no allowing money to do the talking.'

'Except when rich Moroccan businessmen want a favour doing.'

Jason shook his head. 'No favours. Funding. The Firm can't operate on the level it does without benefactors behind it. Those benefactors are chosen extremely carefully, and are acutely aware that they get nothing in return except a warm, fuzzy feeling that they're doing the right thing.'

Sam laughed. 'Now you're telling me there are millionaires and billionaires who have consciences and don't want to play the system?'

'I absolutely am. There are two types of people with money, Sam. Some hoard it offshore and others set up charitable trusts.'

'Let me guess. Those trusts lead straight to The Firm's coffers.'

'Oh, it's a little more complicated than that.'

'Like I said, I don't want to know.'

'Alright,' Jason said chuckling. 'Well, good luck for tonight.'

Sam sighed. 'We're going to need more than luck.'

'You'll be fine. We're going to take these fuckers down, Sam. You mark my words. I know we will. We have to.'

Sam looked at his friend for a moment. 'There's more to this, isn't there? For you, I mean. It's not just Queen and country, is it?' He could have sworn he saw a slight uneasy movement in Jason's eyes.

'What do you mean?' Jason asked, more a statement than a question.

'This is all to do with Penny, isn't it?'

Jason took a deep breath. 'Sam, I can separate my work and private life perfectly well.'

Sam wanted to suggest that wouldn't be so easy if they were one and the same, but he thought better of it. This was clearly territory Jason didn't want to go into, so he kept quiet. 'Alright. Sorry. Like you say, I'm sure it'll be fine.'

Jason nodded, and turned to leave. As he got to the front door, he stopped and pulled his phone out of his pocket. A few seconds later, he turned back to Sam, holding his phone in front of him, a photo of what looked to Sam to be a Muslim man on the screen.

Sam narrowed his eyes. 'Who's that?' he asked.

'This is the man who's responsible for Penny's death. Azim al Huq. He's the guy who's in Sullivan's employ. While he's useful, anyway. Sooner or later he'll be the fall guy, you mark my words. Everyone is eventually. You'll find what you find, Sam, but this is the guy I want. This is our link.'

47

Dee had been known to arrive early at work on occasion, but clocking in at five-forty in the morning was a new one on her.

She already had her excuses lined up. She'd tell anyone who asked that she'd been suffering with insomnia recently — possibly as a result of the closeness of the Westminster bombing — and work was helping to take her mind off things. What was the harm in coming in early and getting more work done?

Security was tighter overnight, but there was technically nothing stopping anyone from coming and going at any time, and some departments even operated night-shift working, particularly if there were ongoing projects with overseas territories or the Foreign and Commonwealth Office.

If the operation didn't work, she'd be on a shortlist of people who were in the office at the time everything went wrong. She already felt sure she'd been identified as someone of interest, so the risks to her personally were huge. It still wasn't enough to stop her, though. Things were moving too quickly and too dramatically to just sit back and do nothing. She would put her life on the line to protect the liberty of others if that was what it took.

She'd seen the movement of traffic over the past couple of decades and it had concerned her greatly. Things had moved even faster over the past year or two, and it seemed Britain was headed for full-on jingoistic nationalism. With that came the implicit acceptance of racism and prejudice, handily packaged up over the past few years as 'political correctness gone mad' — a favourite term used by those who took umbrage at not being allowed to be an arsehole to other people.

She'd watched as the mythical Schrödinger's Immigrant — those who simultaneously managed to 'steal our jobs' and at the same time somehow 'sit at home on benefits' — became the scapegoat for the failings of the Establishment. She'd seen the public schoolboys, investment bankers and distant cousins of the Queen proclaim themselves to be the voices of the working class and declare how they were the anti-Establishment voice of Britain. And the public had lapped it up.

It spoke of change. It spoke of hope. It didn't matter how clearly it was absolute bollocks — the instigators and protagonists positively revelled in how blatant and obvious they could be in their shenanigans, knowing how powerful and all-consuming the 'taking back control' message was. It was deep. It was hypnotic. It was perfect.

She could quite easily see how so many people thought the way they did. She didn't blame them one bit. She'd seen the lies and misinformation they'd been fed. She'd seen how they'd been polarised, how they'd turn on anyone who had a different view to them and declare even stronger allegiance to the new brand of politicos who'd legitimised their voice.

But that wouldn't stop her from fighting the rising tide of

hatred. It would only make her speak out more loudly, more vociferously. Because as soon as hatred won, as soon as those tax-dodging investment bankers and public schoolboys gained control and were able to ditch the working man, the game was over for everyone. What had happened to respect and being nice to other people?

She held on tight to the USB stick in her jacket pocket as she waited for the lift to take her to the floor of her office. There, she'd log on to her own computer and get a few administrative tasks done before heading to the server room at just the right time.

Sam had told her the best ways to avoid being spotted on the way. At least, he'd told her what had been the best ways before his dismissal. There was no way of knowing what they'd changed since then.

The reset was due to occur at six o'clock, the updates having been installing since the early hours. Dee knew the next fifteen minutes would feel like an age.

But, slowly and gradually, ten of them passed, and she made her way to the server room, nervous but excited. She stopped at the door and entered the access code Sam had given her.

This was the first hurdle. There was no way of knowing if they'd changed the access code. It wasn't something they usually did when a member of staff left — mainly because that person would no longer be able to gain access to the building in the first place — but they were now living in unprecedented times.

She pressed the green button after entering the digits, and was greeted by the sound of falling latches. She pulled down on the handle, swung open the heavy door and entered the chilly room.

Amongst the blinking lights and sea of cables, Dee located

the rack Sam had detailed to her and waited. She watched the clock on her smartphone, knowing it was synchronised to the same atomic clock as the servers, every second passing in front of her eyes, mentally calculating how long she had left until she had to plunge the USB stick into the right socket and let Sam's program do its job.

***

Sam took another slug of coffee and watched his mobile phone intently. He was waiting for Dee's call, for the moment she told him the USB drive was in situ and he could attempt to connect.

The window was tiny. Three seconds at most, Sam estimated. There was really only one shot at getting this right.

Each server would restart a few seconds after the last, making sure there was always at least 50% server capacity running at any given time. To anyone accessing information at that point, they might possibly notice a slight slowdown as the other servers took up the slack, but to all intents and purposes they'd remain online throughout.

The server Dee was manipulating was the first to restart. If for some reason she missed the window, she'd still technically have a chance with the last, although the likelihood was the first attempted connection would flag up as a security breach and it would be game over anyway.

They couldn't risk mucking it up. He'd briefed Dee as much as he could, but no amount of preparation could beat the importance of the next few seconds.

***

05.59.00.

One minute left.

Dee swallowed hard, chastising herself for coming here too early. What if she was caught? There was no-one around, but she still shouldn't have taken the risk. Each second seemed to take a year to pass.

She could hear her own heartbeat above the sound of the spinning drives and humming power supply units. She tried to calm her breathing, telling herself she needed to relax if she was going to get this right. Shaky hands would not do.

05.59.10.

She looked again at the rack Sam had identified to her. It was definitely the right one. The serial number matched up. The USB port was exactly where Sam had said it was. She looked at the USB stick in her hand and made sure it was the right way round. There could be no fumbling or getting this wrong.

05.59.20.

She ran through the plan again in her mind. At exactly six o'clock, she'd insert the drive. The servers would begin to restart, and within three seconds the firewall would be protecting them again. Thirty seconds or so after that, they'd be fully operational and back in business.

05.59.30.

Dee called Sam. They didn't want to keep their phone line open for too long, but at the same time they didn't want to risk the call not connecting at first and missing their window altogether.

Sam answered on the first ring. Dee switched back to the Clock app and watched the seconds drop. She updated Sam on the live time.

05.59.40.
Twenty seconds left.

Sam wiped his hands on the front of his dressing gown, trying to remain calm and wondering just how nervous Dee would be. She'd always been the cool, calm and collected one of the two of them but he knew there was no way even she would be taking this in her stride.

He knew she was in the zone, though. The only words they'd said had been hellos, followed by Dee updating him on the live time.

'Are you alright?' he asked.

'Fine,' Dee said, swallowing hard.

05.59.50.

'Ten seconds.'

'Right. Got the drive ready?'

'Milimetres from the socket.'

'Alright. Sit tight.'

Dee counted down.

'Five. Four. Three. Two. One.'

She slid the USB drive into the socket and waited. Nothing seemed to be happening.

'Should there be some sort of noise? A light?' Dee asked.

'They'll make noise when they restart,' Sam answered.

'They aren't doing anything.'

'Give it a second.'

'I've given it plenty,' she said, just as the first server started to whirr and rise in volume. 'Wait. I think they're doing something.'

'Alright. Great. Stand by.'

Sam pressed the button on his laptop, knowing that the whirring of the servers meant they had initiated their reboot process. This was the three-second window.

Server not found.

Too soon.

He pressed the button again. This time, he was greeted with a symbol showing him the program was attempting to initiate a connection.

When a new message appeared on the screen, it took him a moment to digest it. It wasn't the one he'd expected.

Access denied.

'Sam? Has it done it?' Dee asked, waiting for his response.

'Uh, I don't know. I don't think so. No.'

'What? What's gone wrong?'

'I don't know. Everything seems fine in theory. I can't see why it wouldn't connect. There must be a problem somewhere. Hang on.'

As Dee closed her eyes and tried to keep herself calm, slowing the pulsing and pounding of the blood in her ears, she felt a hand on her shoulder.

48

Dee was thankful she'd been given some preparation by The Firm on what to do if ever she found herself in difficulty. In effect, it consisted of keeping quiet and waiting for strings to be pulled behind the scenes. That didn't make her situation any more comfortable, though.

She'd been arrested and taken to a high-security holding area on suspicion of domestic terrorism. Specialist counter-terrorism officers had been assigned to the case, and it seemed to Dee that they'd been waiting a long time for the right moment to pounce. This hadn't just been a case of catching her on CCTV early that morning.

They weren't daft. Holding her under anti-terrorism legisla-tion meant she could be detained for much longer than she could for any other crime before either being charged or released.

As far as Dee saw it, there was very little chance of her being released. There could be no doubt as to her involvement in the subversion of the Home Office's computer systems. The only grey area would be with regards to her motive, but she could hardly claim to be an investigative journalist. Even if she could, she'd be on shaky ground.

Sullivan's followers would brand her a 'domestic terrorist', hell-bent on halting the rise of Sullivan's party and his now almost certain grip on power. Certain newspapers would probably go so far as to brand her a 'Marxist' for not being too keen on blind hate-filled nationalism, and Sullivan himself would use Dee as perfect evidence of why he was justified in ridding the civil service of those he deemed to be subversive to the national interest. When he claimed he was on the side of 'the people', he could get away with anything.

But for now, Dee's more immediate focus was on seeing out her initial interview with the counter-terrorism police and regaining her freedom. That last part, however, would be down to her colleagues at The Firm.

Would they throw her under the bus? She sincerely hoped not, but she could never be entirely sure.

She couldn't be sure, either, if the counter-terrorism officers interviewing her later that morning were just doing their job or whether they too had drunk the Michael Sullivan Kool Aid.

'Can you confirm your full name for me?' the first officer asked her.

Dee didn't answer.

'Can you confirm that your full name is Dee Rhiannon Edgewood?'

Again, Dee didn't answer.

'Dee, why did you take part in an attempted cyber attack on government computer systems?'

Silence.

'Why did you work with Sam Barker to try to install covert software on Home Office servers, Dee?'

She didn't reply, and tried not to show her surprise at the mention of Sam's name. She knew they'd try to drop things like this into the interview in an attempt to shock her into speaking. They likely knew about her previous relationship with Sam and would use him as leverage in trying to get her to speak. But she wouldn't fall for it.

'Sam was let go from his job at the Home Office recently, wasn't he? Would you say he was angry and resentful, perhaps?'

Dee tried to block out their words, focusing instead on thinking about other things and waiting for the cogs to be put into motion by The Firm. She had to keep the faith that they'd get her out of here one way or another.

'Has Sam been behaving differently since the Westminster bombing? I understand he was in the station when the bomb went off. That would be enough to give anyone some rather disturbed thoughts, don't you think?'

As hard as she tried, she was struggling to block out their words. But she couldn't let them win.

'You'd be able to see if he'd changed, wouldn't you? You know each other pretty well. Intimately, I understand. Do you have anything to say about that?'

Dee didn't speak, but the second counter-terrorism officer did.

'This isn't some sort of Bonnie and Clyde adventure, Dee. This isn't you and him against the system. This could be considered by some to amount to treason.'

Dee was not going to be riled. Even though her internal thoughts might be different, there was no way in hell she was going to show these bastards that they were affecting her.

'Dee, we can help you,' the first counter-terrorism officer said. 'If you tell us who else is involved in your operation, we can ensure your sentence is as light as possible. We can't guarantee you won't go down, but you'll have a significantly easier time of it. There are things we can do. We know you're not the ringleader. You're an HR Manager. No disrespect. We know Sam Barker isn't exactly the head honcho, either. But if you lead us to the right people, we can make sure you're both looked after.'

Dee wanted to lean over the table and punch him right in the mouth, but she managed to resist.

'We know there are people out there who can tempt you into different ways of thinking. Conspiracy theories are very attractive. You can see a conspiracy anywhere if you really want to. But the British government has, and always has had, the interests of the British people at its heart. Deep down you know that, don't you?'

The second officer decided to interrupt the silence.

'You don't have to speak, but if you remain silent you will be going down for this. We've got our computer forensics guys going through that program as we speak. They'll be able to trace everything. We've got you bang to rights. And you know why? Because you've been shafted. You've been completely let down by the people who promised to protect you. Where are they? Why did they let you end up in this position? You've been thrown under the bus, Dee. You and Sam Barker. You're nothing to them. As far as they're concerned, you no longer exist. Why on earth would you want to help them?'

Dee gritted her teeth, desperate not to let their words get to her, but with every passing minute she too wondered why the hell she was still in here, and why the right levers hadn't been pulled to get her out.

49

Sam'd had a pretty good idea as to what had happened when the call dropped, and he knew it was only a matter of time before they traced things back to him.

Travers had called him within the hour to explain that Dee had been arrested by counter-terrorism police. Sam knew immediately that meant they'd been watched. There was no way they'd just happened to be passing at six o'clock that morning. They'd been lying in wait, knowing what they'd planned. But how? Had they been bugged? Was there someone, somewhere along the line who'd betrayed them?

There were many questions that needed answering, and Travers had promised Sam they'd be answered. He'd also given Sam his word that The Firm would do all they could to secure Dee's release, but that it would take time. That told Sam the higher powers hadn't foreseen Dee's arrest and had no idea they were being watched. That worried him.

He knew he had to keep the faith somehow, but it wasn't that easy. He'd spent his whole life having complete and utter belief in his country and his government, only to have that shattered within the past few weeks. Desolate and alone, he'd put his faith in The Firm, but now he was starting to wonder just how much he could trust them to protect him.

He'd heard of people declaring themselves to be 'politically homeless' before, but to find himself completely without identity or basic safety was a feeling more horrific than Sam could ever have expected or imagined.

It had been a few hours since Dee's arrest and, so far, Sam hadn't had any knocks at the door. He was sure they'd come at some point, but he also suspected they'd make him sit and sweat for as long as possible first.

For now, there was nothing he could do. Travers had told him to stay put, not to do anything drastic or silly. For now, he was as safe as he could be. If he attempted to run, there was no doubt he'd be arrested and taken in on similar charges to Dee. All he could do for the moment was lay low and keep calm. Easier said than done.

Sam decided he needed some distraction, so he sat down on his sofa and switched on the TV. It wasn't something he tended to do to relax, much preferring to sink into a book or do something more constructive, but right now he needed the mind-numbing nothingness of just staring at a screen, letting everything on it do the work so he didn't have to.

The TV was tuned to BBC One, and Sam soon realised it was showing the build-up to the unveiling of the Westminster memorial. He was glad he hadn't agreed to go. How could he, after this morning's events? He'd have been constantly looking over his shoulder, wondering if and when he was going to be ambushed by counter-terrorism police or Sullivan's people. And who was to say they weren't one and the same?

The build-up to the unveiling was almost nauseating. The presenters, plucked from the evening news, spoke sombrely about the events which had led up to today, had run through the names and pictures of those who died in the attack and had paid tribute to those fighting overseas against Islamist militants. There had been no mention of the fact that Muqatili Alhuriyati didn't exist.

There were interviews with the artist, Khalid Saleem and the businessman who'd funded the project, Mohammad Yousuf Zaher. They spoke eloquently about the need for the population to realise that the majority of Muslims were extending the hand of friendship, and wanted to live as one in the same community. No minority of terrorists should seek to undermine that, they said, no matter how small.

The coverage cut to a short piece on the making of the monument, mentioning that it had been constructed in an empty hangar at the mostly disused Smithfield Aerodrome, after an anonymous businessman had donated the space rent-free.

Sam's blood ran cold. Why did Smithfield Aerodrome ring a bell? Where had he heard that name before?

Dee's voice played in his head.

There was a girl who went to the police and told them a group of men had raped her at the old Smithfield Aerodrome. It was hushed up. The girl was made out to be a liar. Her parents tried going to the papers, and somehow that got back to the top brass. Twenty-four hours later, dad dies in a car accident. Hit and run. The other driver was never found. This is what we're dealing with here.

As Sam's brain started to piece things together, bit by bit, he watched the screen as it showed footage of the construction of the monument inside Smithfield Aerodrome over the past weeks, and the members of the Muslim community who'd pledged support and expertise in building it.

And that was when he recognised Azim al Huq.

50

Sam tried desperately to control the shaking of his hands as he called Tom Travers. The phone seemed to take an age to connect, before dropping out.

He tried again.

Nothing.

The panic was now rising in his chest as he realised what was going to happen. It was all too convenient. The memorial piece to those who'd died in the Westminster bombing, designed by a Muslim artist and bankrolled by a Muslim businessman, had been constructed at Smithfield Aerodrome — a location with known links to Michael Sullivan. Azim al Huq was there. There was no mistaking him. It was clear to Sam what had happened.

It now seemed blindingly obvious to him that the Aerodrome had been given rent-free to the artist and his team for one reason only: so that someone close to Sullivan could tamper with it, pack it full of explosives, to ensure it would cause maximum damage and once again point the finger of blame for an act of terrorism at the Muslim population.

That was it. It had to be. Sullivan and his people were minutes away from executing another false-flag attack, and this one would be by far the biggest yet.

He looked out of his window onto the street below. In his area of London, everything seemed to be business as usual. But he knew that a little further into town things would be very different indeed.

He peered through the curtains, unsure what he was looking for, but feeling desperate. Was someone watching him? Were they getting a kick out of knowing that he'd realised what was about to happen? Was that why they hadn't come for him yet? Did they want him to see this unfold piece by piece?

He tried calling Travers again, but the phone still wouldn't connect. He tried dialling Jason's number, but ran into the same problem. Had someone cut his phone off?

'Fuck!'

Sam's breath caught in his throat as he watched the TV screen. Four black cars were coasting through the streets of London, on their way to Westminster. One of them, Sam knew, contained Her Majesty the Queen.

A surge of panic rose within him. It was all starting to make sense.

Of course. It was the ultimate opportunity for Sullivan. Another attack was another attack, but this one would be almost perfect.

It would be an attack on a memorial service and unveiling of a monument for the victims of the largest terrorist attack to hit London. It had the double sting of appearing to be a Muslim conspiracy, with both the artist and the benefactor being of Islamic faith. And one of the closest people to the monument would be by far its most prominent victim: the Queen.

For Sullivan, it would be perfect. Poetic. Who would suspect the country's biggest patriot of committing treason? At her age she probably didn't have long left anyway, and her death at the hands of terrorists would send insurmountable shock-waves through society. Sullivan would be propelled to power, with a stranglehold so strong he'd lead the country for a genera-tion. There, he'd have carte blanche to act however he wanted and to further whichever corrupt causes he wished.

But what could he do? Dee was being held by counter-terrorism police. He had no way of contacting Jason or Tom Travers and, in any case, Jason had told him that he and Travers were going to Morocco.

Should he call the police? How could he when he didn't know who to trust? And who would believe a man under suspi-cion for domestic terrorism phoning the police to say he thought the Queen was about to be blown up by a bomb?

He looked at the hoards of people on TV. Hundreds of thousands lined the streets. God only knew how many would die. Thousands, possibly more. It would make the Westminster bombing a mere mention in dispatches when it came to the history books.

Feeling the bile rising from the pit of his stomach, he ran to his kitchen and vomited into the sink, retching hard until there was nothing more to come.

It wasn't the shock of what was about to happen that had caused that reaction; it was the realisation that he was the only man who could stop it. And there was only one way to do it.

51

Before he allowed his anxiety to stop him, Sam had put on his shoes, left his flat and taken the steps down to street level three at a time.

He darted around the corner onto Lambeth Palace Road, desperate for a break in the traffic so he could cross over onto the other side. Spotting what he considered to be a reasonable gap, he ran out between a double-decker bus and a black cab, horns blaring as he got to the other side of the road in relative safety.

The traffic was heavy, but moving — except for anything heading in the direction of Westminster Bridge. He rounded the corner onto the bridge road and tried to pick up as much pace as he could, his chest burning as he exercised muscles he hadn't used in a long time. At the other end of the bridge was Westminster Station, with Parliament Square Garden — and the memorial — almost directly opposite. He was seconds away.

As the Thames opened up on either side of him, he spotted the police cordon on the other side of the bridge, just beyond the growing throngs of people.

He slowed down, pushing his way through the crowds, his head buzzing. This wasn't where he wanted to be.

Too much going on.

Too many people.

No control.

He pushed forward regardless, telling himself he had no choice.

The fluorescent arm of the policeman darted out in front of him.

'Sorry buddy, no more at the moment. Crowd control. You'll have to move back.'

Sam's heart sank. He looked at his watch. The memorial was due to be unveiled in just a few minutes. There wasn't time to waste.

He turned around and pushed his way back through the crowds, shouting at people to move as he sprinted back towards the south side of the river, almost sobbing with desperation.

As the bridge touched land, Sam darted right and ran down the stairs to the South Bank. As he approached the halfway point on the stairs, he landed awkwardly, his ankle twisting beneath him as he fell to an agonising heap on the stone platform.

Wincing and groaning in pain, he yelped as a Chinese tourist helped him to his feet. Ignoring the woman's pleas to call him an ambulance, Sam shook his head and tried to put pressure on his ankle.

It hurt like fucking hell. The pain shot up the side of his leg and almost blew his hip out. It made him feel sick. But he had no option. He had to go on.

He hobbled down the steps, each bolt of pain numbing his leg slightly more, until he'd become so desensitised to the agony and so flooded with adrenaline, he was able to half-jog half-limp his way along the South Bank, past St Thomas's Hospital and Lambeth Palace, to the foot of Lambeth Bridge.

Putting both hands on the railing beside him, he hauled himself up the stone steps, rising above the Thames and onto the bridge itself. Here, the traffic was a little quieter but still busier than normal, the whole of central London having been brought to a relative standstill by the day's events.

Reaching the roundabout at the end of the bridge, Sam turned right onto Millbank and continued to make his way up the road as quickly as his injured ankle would let him. He'd worry about the damage later. For now, there was far more at stake.

As Millbank opened up onto Abingdon Street, the crowds began to grow thick again, a sea of people right up to the front of the Houses of Parliament.

The parks — Abingdon Street Garden, The College Garden and beyond them the grounds of St Margaret's Church — looked even busier, so Sam decided his best option was to stick to the road and pavements.

He knew he couldn't appear too desperate. He had to stop running, had to stop looking like a man on a mission.

But what could he do? Did he find a police officer or security worker? Could he trust them? Would he be taken seriously? They were hardly going to call the whole thing off and bundle the Queen into the back of a limo and drive her away just because a random guy in the street told them there was a bomb threat, were they?

The enormous crowd seemed to throb in front of him, and it felt as though ten thousand eyes were upon him.

He squeezed his eyes shut and tried to block them out, tried to tell himself they didn't matter. He was here for a reason. He was going to help them, going to save them. He could deal with all that later.

Sam felt himself shaking and sweating — he didn't know whether through exertion or anxiety. His heart began to pound faster and faster, and in that moment he knew it wasn't the journey that had done it.

As he opened his eyes and looked at the crowds in front of him, Sam started to notice the sides of his vision closing in, turning black.

His last sensation before losing consciousness was that of someone grabbing hold of his arm.

52

The sensation of the cold brick wall against his back soon brought Sam round.

The face he saw in front of him was not one he expected.

'Tom?'

Travers stood firm in front of him, holding Sam up against the wall, a look of deep concern in his eyes.

'You're in Morocco,' Sam said.

'I was. Briefly. But now I'm not. Believe me, I'd far rather be there than here right now.'

'What's going on, Tom?'

Travers stood back, allowing Sam to stand on his own one-and-a-half legs.

'I think that's a question you need to answer, Sam. What are you playing at?'

'I... I've got to stop it. Now.'

'Never a truer word spoken.'

'My phone. It's been cut off.'

'I know. We did it.'

'You? Why?'

'Because you're a liability, Barker. A security risk at best. At worst a threat to our very existence. You're damn lucky you're not at the bottom of the Thames right now.'

'What are you talking about?'

'The lost laptop. The sacking. Leading Dee into the arms of counter-terrorism. Not been a great few weeks for you, Sam.'

'Tom, we can sort this all out later. I've got to stop the unveiling. Something's going to happen. Something big.'

Travers narrowed his eyes. 'What do you mean?'

'Sullivan's people have put a bomb inside the memorial piece. The statue. Whatever you call it. It's going to explode at any moment. All these people could be killed. We have to move them!'

Travers looked at him for a moment, then let out a small snort.

'I never should have listened to Dee and Jason in the first place.'

'You've got to believe me!' Sam pleaded. 'Tom, I'm telling the truth.'

'And you discovered this how? Using the computer program you couldn't even install at the Home Office? Or the security credentials you no longer possess? Sam, you can barely get into your own flat at the moment, so how do you expect me to believe you've managed to unlock some secret conspiracy? You've lost the plot. You're not strong enough for this. Up here, I mean,' he said, his index finger jabbing into Sam's left temple. 'The whole thing's sent you mad.'

'Tom, please. That monument was put together at Smithfield Aerodrome. The land's known to be linked to Sullivan and the Wonderland paedophile ring. You must already know that.

Look at the facts. Muslim artist, Muslim benefactor. Al Huq was even there on the TV footage!'

Travers's eyes narrowed. 'How do you know that name?'

'Listen, Tom. It's the ideal opportunity for Sullivan to prove his warped view that Islam is a threat to Britain. It's perfect for him.'

'We act based on evidence only, Sam. What do you have to back this up other than two plus two equalling five?'

Sam sighed.

Travers nodded slowly. 'Just as I thought.'

Before Sam could reply, the noise of the crowd rose to rapturous cheering and applause as the black limousine carrying Her Majesty the Queen came to a slow stop in front of Parliament Square Garden.

53

'Tom, please. At least call Jason. He's known me for years. He'll know I'm telling the truth.'

Travers shook his head. 'We're past dealing with character references here, Sam.'

'Listen, Jason knows me better than anybody. You *know* he's trustworthy. That's why he works for you. He's one of your best guys. You and I haven't got off to the best start, I know. But you trust Jason. You know you do. And if you do, you *have* to tell him. You need to have confidence in his judgement, even if you haven't got any in mine.'

Travers shook his head again, before grimacing and pushing Sam back up against the wall. 'You just don't get it, do you, Barker? We can't have people like you working with us. Jason told us you were cool, calm and collected. But you're just a hothead in disguise. You're a loose cannon. A liability. You can't even keep your cool sitting at home in your own flat, never mind working on issues of international security. And now you want me to call your friend for a character reference? Do you have any idea how fucking stupid you sound?'

Sam tried to remain calm. He knew arguing with Tom was only going to make things worse and reinforce his view that Sam was a loose cannon.

'Alright,' he said. 'Let's say you act on what I say and get those people to safety. If you're right and I'm wrong, it's been a bit of a cock-up. It's inconvenienced a few people and we both look daft. If I'm right and you're wrong and we don't act, hundreds, potentially thousands of people — including our head of state — are going to be killed. Tell me it's worth the gamble.'

Tom looked at him for a few moments, his eyes narrowing. Then he turned and walked off into the crowd.

Sam's heart sank. This was it. It was all over.

A little further up Abingdon Street, Her Majesty the Queen smiled as she greeted the crowds gathered in front of Big Ben, before making her way up the steps towards the stage.

54

As soon as the Queen began to speak, Sam knew he didn't have long. There could only be seconds left at best.

He didn't know how long it had been since Tom had rejected his pleas and walked off into the crowds — everything was a blur. He could hear the pounding of blood in his ears, feel the rising need to be sick, see his arms and legs shaking as his anxiety grew and grew.

Without thinking, he burst out of the alleyway and pushed his way up Abingdon Street as quickly as he could.

As he got closer to the stage, the crowds grew thicker. He was barely fifty yards away now, but the resistance of the swarm of people slowed him down to a near standstill. It struck him that were the bomb to detonate now, he would almost certainly be one of those who'd be seriously injured at the very least.

He tried to push his way through a cluster of bodies, but was hauled back by a man at least twice his size. These were Londoners in mourning. Tens of thousands of them. They were in no mood to be pushed around, either figuratively or literally.

Looking over the shoulders to his right, he thought he

spotted a security officer. Was that someone he could trust? Were they in Sullivan's pay? He had no way of knowing, but it had to be worth the risk. The alternative was too much to bear.

He glanced back towards the stage and caught sight of the Queen. Just as he planned to start his push through the crowd towards the security staff, he watched as a man in a dark suit approached her and whispered in her ear, before shuffling her off the stage.

Was this all part of the plan? What was going on? Was the idea to get the Queen out of the way just before the explosion, keeping her safe but making it look like she'd been the target all along?

Sam was starting to realise there was no way of predicting how many steps ahead Sullivan and his people were. They seemed to have the whole game planned out before anyone else even knew they were playing.

As the crowd began to murmur and rumble, wondering what was going on, a voice came over the loudspeaker asking them to move quickly and calmly in the direction of Millbank and Lambeth Bridge.

The crowds, sensing something was amiss, decided to move quickly but not very calmly, almost stampeding past Sam and to the south.

And that was when he felt the explosion.

THE GUARDIAN

28TH JUNE

LONDON UNDER ATTACK: WHAT HAPPENED?

The silence from officials over the cause of the latest explosion to rock the capital has been deafening this week, with police and government officials still unwilling or unable to say what happened.

The explosion that killed four people and left dozens of others injured was initially believed to be a terrorist attack, but communication from law enforcement agencies has since dried up, leading many to wonder the true cause.

Some tabloids have — perhaps predictably — declared this to be evidence of an 'Establishment cover-up' designed to protect the Muslim community from the sorts of retaliatory attacks that were seen following the Westminster Underground bombing.

Others have been more reticent to point the finger of blame, noting that the Muqatili Alhuriyati terrorist group had not yet admitted it was responsible. Previous attacks committed by

Muqatili Alhuriyati have seen them admit responsibility within hours.

There has been speculation that the explosion may have been accidental. Television coverage of the event appears to show the detonation originating in the vicinity of the 'One' monument, although some have declared that it shows the explosion happening just below the stage.

If accidental, it will likely be some time before we find out what really happened. However, the complete silence from the authorities over whether it was indeed an accident or some form of deliberate terrorist attack has served only to fuel further conspiracy theories.

At a time of deep political and social unrest in Britain, this newspaper asks whether it is responsible to allow these theories and politically-charged speculation to fill the void left by any official explanation — no matter how vague or temporary.

We understand that pointing the finger of blame at this stage would not be helpful, particularly if it is still unknown who or what is accountable, but allowing blame to ferment where no responsibility lies could easily cause further irreparable damage to our social fabric in a way which no level of ballistic violence could ever hope to achieve.

55

Sam winced as he stood to make himself a cup of tea. Although he hadn't sustained any serious injuries other than busting his ankles on the steps, he was still bloodied and bruised, and felt as though he'd been through a war zone.

He'd been amazed at how quickly the Firm's machine had whirred into action, both on the day of the attack and after.

How Travers had got word to the right people so quickly in order to minimise the devastation, Sam had no idea. He didn't want to ask. Travers had seemed hell-bent on not believing him, and he wondered what had changed in those few seconds.

Sullivan himself had gone strangely quiet since the attack. Jason had assured Sam it was being taken care of, and Sam assumed that to mean Sullivan had been apprehended and would in some way face justice for both Westminster attacks.

The media storm was growing, though, and people were demanding to know who was responsible. Sam didn't know what the official verdict would be — he presumed it wouldn't be announced that the Prime Minister in waiting had been the mastermind behind two terrorist atrocities — including attempted treason —but he couldn't see the public's appetite for a scapegoat going away any time soon. Keeping quiet would only fuel further islamophobia and convince the populace of a government cover-up — although not of the type that had actually occurred.

He was sure he'd find out eventually. For now, though, he didn't care. All he wanted was a quiet life. He'd had enough of the drama, and he looked forward to getting back to normality — whatever that would turn out to be. Lots of things were uncertain in Sam's mind, but that didn't worry him right now.

It pained him to know that people had died in the recent attack, and it haunted him that those deaths could have been avoided if only Travers had listened to him sooner. If only Sam had worked it out sooner. If only he'd not managed to get himself sacked from his job, and had been able to uncover the plot sooner.

If his path had taken a slight deviation at any point, those deaths could have been avoided, and Sam knew they would haunt him for the rest of his life. He knew in his logical mind that he had no reason to bear any responsibility, but logic didn't always come into it.

There were still unanswered questions, though. Who were the corrupt people in the Home Office? What was Sullivan's link to Wonderland? Too many things didn't make sense to Sam, but at the same time he wasn't entirely sure he wanted to know. He'd done his bit. Hopefully now Sullivan would face justice and the rest of the country would find out what he'd done. He knew they wouldn't find out the bulk of it, but he felt sure it would come out in the wash that Sullivan was far from the knight in shining armour many people saw him as.

The time wasn't right, though. No matter what came out,

there was still a huge number of people who wouldn't have their opinions swayed, who would defend Michael Sullivan against even the most egregious of charges, despite the weight of evidence. Because evidence didn't matter any more. Facts were irrelevant. It was what people *felt* that mattered to them, regardless of what was true. And in that sort of world, anything goes.

Although that sort of blind faith worried Sam, he could see where it came from. He'd been there. He'd been unwavering in his patriotism and in the systems of the British Establishment. He'd been steeped in it from a young age. He believed what he'd been fed, and would be the first person to accuse someone of being a conspiracy theorist if they came out with a claim half as outlandish as the things he'd personally witnessed since.

But he was sure that nothing would seem strange or shocking to him anymore.

SULLIVAN STEPS DOWN

Michael Sullivan last night announced his immediate resignation as leader of the opposition due to ill health, sparking panic among his party with a general election imminent.

He subsequently surrendered his seat in the Heath Vale constituency through parliamentary convention of being appointed to the ceremonial post of Steward and Bailiff of the Chiltern Hundreds.

Under British law, elected MPs have no right to resign but can instead opt to apply for the Chiltern Hundreds post or as Steward and Bailiff of the Manor of Northstead — both fictional jobs which carry no salary, but exploit a legal loophole in ancient law which bars the officeholders from being a Member of Parliament.

Sources close to Sullivan stated that they had had no advance notice of his resignation, and many seemed as shocked and surprised as the rest of the nation that the man who just hours earlier seemed certain to become Britain's next Prime

Minister would now be disappearing from the political scene altogether.

Sullivan did not disclose the nature of his illness, although he would not be drawn into speculation regarding a return to politics in the future if his health were to improve.

Sullivan's resignation mirrors other high-profile exits from politics due to illness. Comparisons have already been made in some corners of the media with Winston Churchill's reluctant resignation from office in 1955 through ill health. Two years later, his successor, Sir Anthony Eden, resigned as Prime Minister after doctors warned him his life was at stake if he continued in office. He lived for a further twenty years.

The visit from Jason hadn't been entirely unexpected. Then again, Sam was pretty sure nothing would come as a surprise to him anymore.

There were still questions that needed answering, and Sam was hopeful that Jason might be able to provide some closure, although he doubted it.

'So what did you have to do to get Sullivan to step down?' he asked his friend.

'Don't know what you mean,' Jason replied, in mock denial.

'He doesn't have an illness, does he? Not a physical one, anyway.'

'I'm not his doctor, Sam.'

'You didn't happen to mention Wonderland to him, then?'

'I didn't personally mention anything to him. I've never spoken to the man. Now, why don't you be a good boy and pop the kettle on?'

'There's still something bugging me,' Sam said, once he'd made them both a pot of tea and sat down in his living room.

'We were compromised. Me and Dee. Someone knew what we were doing. There's no way that was just unlucky.'

'I agree,' Jason replied. 'We've got our suspicions. Leave it with us.'

'It was Frank, wasn't it?' Sam said.

'Like I said, leave it with us. We don't want to jump the gun. And in any case, sometimes it's strategically useful to leave someone in place, especially if we can follow leads from them.'

'And what about my job? Will I still have one? Am I meant to just go back to work, knowing there's someone there who's playing for the other side and is out to get me? Is this whole suspension thing going to stack up? What's the deal?'

Jason took a slow sip of his tea, before gently placing the cup back on its saucer. 'That'll all sort itself out in good time. I wouldn't worry about it, personally. Of course, it's in our best interests that things are smoothed over and that you still have access to government information, but I have the feeling that might be a bit difficult to arrange now. Especially while we've still got enemies on the inside.'

'How the hell am I meant to not worry about that?' Sam asked.

'Because you've proven yourself useful to us in plenty of ways as it is. There are a number of ways in which you can help The Firm, Sam. You might not see it yourself, but in many ways you're the ideal person for more than one job.'

Sam had no real inclination to do any more work for The Firm, but at the same time he knew there was no way he would ever be able to put it behind him. It wasn't the sort of thing he could just do as a one-off. He was already tainted. There was no going back. But that didn't mean he had to like it. 'Like what?' he asked.

'There are still some missing links,' Jason said. 'Look at Sullivan and al Huq. There's a link there, without a doubt, but we don't know what it is. Something is missing. Sullivan's far too slippery to work with al Huq directly. There's someone else. Someone in the middle. A missing link.'

'Frank?'

Jason shook his head. 'No. Our man on the inside, if it is him — and I'm not saying it is — is playing another role. He's been the fixer. We're looking for the go-between. The distance. The one who's been making sure Sullivan's hands were kept clean. His pair of gloves, if you will. That person is still out there somewhere.'

'And you want me to find him,' Sam said flatly.

'Oh, I'm not suggesting you disappear off with a raincoat, a trilby and a magnifying glass, don't worry.' Sam had to chuckle to himself. He was long past worrying. 'But you have an important role to play for The Firm, Sam. You can help change the world. Ensure justice prevails. Fairness. Equality. What you've done has helped change the course of history already, Sam. You might well have helped save the future of our nation. But there's a long way to go yet.'

MICHAEL SULLIVAN FOUND DEAD

Michael Sullivan, the former leader of the opposition, has been found dead at his home in Surrey.

Sullivan retired from politics last week citing ill health, a move which surprised many as he had been widely expected to win the upcoming general election and become Britain's next Prime Minister.

Although no official cause of death has yet been given, a neighbour of Mr Sullivan's told this newspaper his death was not through ill health, but instead suggested that the former leader of the opposition had chosen to end his own life rather than succumb to the condition with which he had recently been diagnosed.

His death seems likely to send shockwaves through British politics, with his party still in the process of electing his successor — the person who will likely become the next Prime Minister.

Polling conducted earlier this week suggests a slowdown for

Sullivan's former party, though, with political commentators suggesting that their polling position had been down to Sullivan's own popularity rather than that of the party itself. The polls will be seen as a boost to the government, who may now believe all is not lost in the upcoming election and that they could salvage some of the dozens of seats they'd been widely expected to lose.

57

Although life would never go back to normal, Sam would always be a man who thrived on routine — and he certainly wasn't going to give up his Friday night visits to the pub.

He shared a knowing look with Dee as they sat down in their corner booth and chewed the fat, trying desperately in front of Lucy to make it sound as if their week had been dull.

'Is your mum okay now?' Lucy asked Dee.

Dee felt guilty for doing so, but telling Lucy she'd had to visit Wales unexpectedly in order to tend to her sick mother was the first excuse that had come to mind. It was certainly a lot easier than explaining that she'd been in prison.

Sam was keen to ask her about that, but he knew he'd have to wait until Lucy was out of earshot. This was the first opportunity the pair had had to speak since her release.

'She's fine,' Dee said. 'Doing much better, by all accounts.'

'That's great. Amazing how quickly these things can turn around, isn't it?'

Dee and Sam shared another look.

'Yes, it is,' Dee said, smiling.

'Any news on the job front?' Lucy said, turning to Sam.

'Nothing yet. I've a feeling something will crop up pretty soon, though.'

Lucy shrugged. 'I guess if Sullivan's out of the picture, there's every chance the restructuring will be scrapped. They might even have you back.'

Sam forced a smile. 'Maybe. But I doubt it. In any case, I think it's about time for a change. I'm due something new.'

Lucy smiled and rubbed his forearm. 'Never thought I'd hear you say anything like that. Back in two ticks.'

Sam watched Lucy disappear towards the toilets, then turned to Dee.

'Come on, then. Spill. Please tell me you did a Shawshank-style escape. I can just imagine you hacking away at the wall with your nail file.'

Dee laughed. 'If only it was that romantic. Let's just say Travers pulled a few strings. As per usual.'

'What, just like that? You're not getting off that easily. It's connected with Sullivan, isn't it?'

Dee looked towards the toilets to make sure Lucy wasn't on her way back just yet, then leaned in towards him. 'Alright. The Firm turned over the aerodrome. They surveilled it by drone first of all, and used ground penetrating radar to get a deeper look at the site. Turns out there was some sort of underground area where all the Wonderland stuff went on. The place was an Aladdin's cave of paraphernalia. Including photos of the abuse and more than enough evidence of Sullivan's involvement.'

Sam was breathless. 'Jesus Christ.'

'Yup. Still nothing to prove his links to the terrorist attacks. Yet. But we'll get there. There's a missing link we need to iden-tify. He's still one step removed from it all. We'll find them.'

'This evidence. The Wonderland stuff. Is that what was used to get you off?'

'I can neither confirm nor deny that,' Dee said, smiling.

Sam leaned in a little further, his face serious. 'Is that why Sullivan topped himself? He wasn't ill, was he? It's because the evidence was going to be released.'

'Sam...'

'That's it, isn't it? They're holding back the evidence and gave him the easy way out.'

'Don't ask too many questions, Sam. Trust me.'

Sam's eyes narrowed. 'Shit. He didn't actually kill himself, did he? It's just like Abdul, the patsy. They went in and...'

'Sam.'

Dee's eyes flicked upward as Lucy rejoined them in the booth.

'What are you two talking about?' Lucy asked. 'Anything interesting?'

58

Sam knew better than anyone how quickly and irrevocably someone's life could change. His existence had been turned upside down more times than he cared to remember in recent weeks, and he'd reconciled himself to the fact that it wasn't over yet.

The Firm had organised for Sam to be paid a modest salary from one of many companies they had set up in order to mask their operations. As far as anyone else was concerned, Sam was now an official employee of a security systems company. This would provide cover for his earnings and ensure that everything remained above board — on paper, at least. It would also give Sam an income, although he couldn't help but feel it was rather less reliable and secure than his job working at the heart of government.

But deep down he knew that was all history. There was no way he'd be able to return to his old job. Not at the moment, anyway. Not while there were still people on the inside who knew — or at the very least suspected — his new role. His new life.

It wasn't a life he'd ever wanted. He still didn't want it. But he knew in his heart of hearts that life could never go back to the way it once was. Some things, some changes, were immovable.

It was fair to say he hadn't stopped thinking about any of this at any point, but it was certainly on his mind as he looked at his mobile phone and saw Jason's name on the screen.

It had been weeks since his friend had been in touch, and he had a funny feeling this wouldn't be a social call.

'Jason. Hi,' Sam said as he answered the phone.

'Morning. How's everything going?'

'Yeah, good. Really enjoying this new job I've got. I'm earning more than I was at the Home Office and I don't have to lift a finger. Can't complain at all. Boss is a fucking arsehole, though.'

'Yeah, well that fucking arsehole's been pretty good to you. I don't recall your last boss letting you spend the best part of a fortnight farting around in Scotland.'

Sam laughed. Jason had a point. In the aftermath of the Westminster incident, Sam had spent twelve nights staying up in Edinburgh near Benji and Leila. He'd been able to relax for the first time in a long time, refamiliarising himself with the city and enjoying the fact that he was a few hundred miles from London. He'd definitely connected with Benji in that time, and it had given him memories he knew he'd never lose. He had, though, managed to squirm out of the upcoming global warming event his son had been trying to get him to attend. He wasn't entirely sure that was his bag.

'Well, what can I say?' Sam replied. 'I had plenty of annual leave left to roll over. And I think I probably deserved it.' It wouldn't be easy to tell Jason he was still far from comfortable with his new life. Deep down, he'd do anything to go back to the way things were before he walked into Westminster station that day.

'No arguments from me,' Jason said. 'Although I hope you're suitably relaxed and reenergised.'

'Why's that?' Sam asked, his heart sinking a little.

'Because we've got a little job for you. How do you fancy another trip to Edinburgh?'

ACKNOWLEDGMENTS

There are lots of things which can derail a plot during the process of writing a book.

It's not unusual for me to have to rewrite an ending or go back and introduce a new story thread just as I thought the process was nearly finished. But never before have I experienced the need to keep reshaping a book because real-life events kept outpacing it.

Such is the peril of writing a political thriller in 2019.

When Steven and I started writing *Absolution*, Brexit had made Britain look a little incompetent at best. As the book began to take shape, our politics took a far more sinister turn.

We were both keen that *Absolution* should not be seen as a political commentary or satire. In original drafts, Michael Sullivan was already Prime Minister, having risen to power on a wave of populism which had largely drowned out common sense and reason. In July 2019 we realised real life had overtaken us.

During the plotting of the book, Steven and I discussed the planned bomb attack at the end occurring at Wimbledon, during London's annual tennis tournament. Barely an hour later, the Italian tennis player Fabio Fognini said 'I wish a bomb would explode on this club'.

The story thread which linked Sullivan to the Wonderland paedophile ring was originally more detailed and formed a much larger part of *Absolution*. A high profile character in the book was seen to testify before losing his life. Then, just as we were putting the finishing touches to this scene, Jeffrey Epstein was found dead in his prison cell after testifying against former members of a paedophile ring.

Some early readers of the book have taken great delight in declaring that Character X is obviously, quite clearly Politician Y. It isn't. In fact, we've taken enormous care not to enter the realms of satire or to base any characters in *Absolution* on real people. The book was completely re-plotted and re-written on more than one occasion in order to avoid just this problem. Unfortunately, real life kept aping us.

We wanted, without being too political, to write a book which would entertain, thrill and make people think. We certainly didn't want to preach, and I sincerely hope we've avoided that. If we've made you feel uneasy about some thoughts or views, good. That is precisely what all good fiction should do.

My biggest thanks have to go to Steven Moore, my wonderful co-author, who continued to smile whilst smashing his head off a brick wall as real life events, illness, full diaries and my own ineptitude continued to get in the way of our progress. Any and all errors are mine.

Thanks also go to Sacha Black, who read early incarnations of *Absolution* and tried not to laugh too hard. Her feedback was invaluable in helping to shape the book you've just read.

To all my readers who've continued to ask me how the series was coming along. Having you there to kick me up the backside is exactly what I need. You're the last people I'd ever want to let down.

To Mark Boutros for his ongoing support and immense knowledge of character and plot. Not only is he a fantastic sounding board, but he also knows a good football team when he sees one, which is more than can be said for Mr Moore.

To Lucy Hayward for her eagle eye and for never holding back in giving her honest feedback. I will forever admire her unswerving determination that my books should be as good as they possibly can be.

To my mum for always being one of my earliest readers and for offering her own feedback and suggestions for improvements. Sorry you have to read so many crime and thriller books.

And last but certainly not least, to my wife, Joanne, for her suggestions in improving the plot and characters, as well as egging me on to get the thing finished. Her support is always greater than she knows.

Adam Croft

Wow. Where to start? I guess there's only one place really. Thus, my heartfelt thanks and appreciation go out to Adam, not only for initially sharing his premise for the Sam Barker thriller series over one too many drinks at the London Book Fair, but later for entrusting me to collaborate with him on the series after those early discussions. Addendum: I notice Croft knocking my football team. Well, buddy, only one of our teams has the word 'Arse' in the name. I rest my case.

As Adam stated in his acknowledgments above, it has been quite a challenging process to reach this point. There have been many obstacles to overcome: British political upheaval, real-world events biting us in our respective plotting butts, time zones (I live in Mexico most of the year, and when I'm up and about slaving over the manuscript Adam was usually found lounging around his country mansion sipping Earl Grey). But now we've finally finished, having navigated all those obstacles to the best of our ability, I can honestly say it's all been worth it.

I'd also like to give my friend and fellow thriller author David Berens a shout out. It was Dave who recommended me to Adam, right around the time Adam and I met at the book fair in London. It was those kind words that set Adam and I on this path together. Thanks, Dave.

Next, like Adam, I'd like to thank Sacha. Over the course of some curt messages and a few straight-talking Skype chats, my direction was focussed and my wrongs, righted. If you're an author and you want to be told things straight, ask Sacha.

Of course, I'd like to thank all the readers out there. Without readers, the words we put into our stories are just that: mere words. Writing a book is often a long, difficult and sometimes painful journey, and to know someone has enjoyed our work makes it all worthwhile. Readers are the reason we write in the first place, and I'm sure I speak for Adam too when I say a huge, heartfelt thank you to anyone who has reached the end of this book.

And finally, an even bigger thank you to my wife Leslie. It's Leslie who got me into this fiction malarkey in the first place, and I'll forever be grateful. On our very first date she challenged me to write a novel. That was in March, 2011. Absolution is my 12th novel to date, and none of those books would have been possible without her unstinting support and confidence-boosting encouragement. They say behind every good man is a great woman. Whoever 'they' are, they're right.

Steven Moore

NOTES FROM THE AUTHORS

ADAM CROFT

To say thank you for reading *Absolution*, I'd like to invite you to my exclusive VIP Club, and give you some of my books and short stories for **free**. All members of my VIP Club have access to free, exclusive books and short stories which aren't available anywhere else.

You'll also get access to all of my new releases at the best possible price before they're available anywhere else. Joining is absolutely FREE and you can leave at any time, no questions asked. To join the club, head to adamcroft.net/vip-club and two free books will be sent to you straight away.

STEVEN MOORE

To sign up and receive Steven's spam-free newsletter, where you'll be the first to learn about his new releases, discounts and competitions, simply visit subscribepage.com/stevenmooreauthor.

As a thank you for subscribing, you'll receive a **free** Hiram Kane novella.

ADAM CROFT

With almost two million books sold to date, Adam Croft is one of the most successful independently published authors in the world, and one of the biggest selling authors of the past few years, having sold books in over 120 different countries.

During the summer of 2016, two of Adam's books hit the USA Today bestseller list only weeks apart, making them two of the most-purchased books in the United States over the summer.

In February 2017, Only The Truth became a worldwide bestseller, reaching storewide number 1 at both Amazon US and Amazon UK, making it the bestselling book in the world at that moment in time. The same day, Amazon's overall Author Rankings placed Adam as the most widely read author in the world, with J.K. Rowling in second place.

Adam has been featured on BBC television, BBC Radio 4, BBC Radio 5 Live, the BBC World Service, The Guardian, The Huffington Post, The Bookseller and a number of other news and media outlets.

In March 2018, Adam was conferred as an Honorary Doctor of Arts, the highest academic qualification in the UK, by the University of Bedfordshire in recognition of his services to literature.

Adam presents the regular crime fiction podcast Partners in Crime with fellow bestselling author Robert Daws.